MW00380969

The Wolves

Joe Gorman

Like Joe Gorman's author page on Facebook

Please add him on Twitter: @JoeJoegorman

Add him on Instagram: josephpatrickgorman

Please add a review on Amazon or Goodreads. Thanks!

Copyright 2018 Joe Gorman

All rights reserved.

Dedicated to my beautiful soul mate, Colleen Mulhern Riccio.

Cover design by Diana Lahr

Edited by Jaime Underwood Harker

(https://www.linkedin.com/in/jharker814/)

Chapter One

Members of a Mexican drug gang based in Sinaloa became frustrated with the challenge of freeing the head of their cartel from a United States maximum security prison. They dispatched a team of narco-terrorists to Sonora to explore the possibility of using ancient Indian sorcery to free him. The cartel's leader, Esteban Gracias, had twice escaped from maximum security prisons in Mexico. Gracias was taken into custody by officers of the U.S. Drug Enforcement Administration in a small Mexican border town near El Paso. He was extradited to New York to face drug trafficking and money laundering charges; if convicted, he would spend the rest of his life in a U.S. federal prison. High-powered American and Mexican attorneys were hired. Despite their best legal efforts, the cartel remained pessimistic about freeing Gracias through judicial avenues, particularly in the highly charged political atmosphere in the United States. Bribery and intimidation of prison guards and their families were futile north of the border. American federal prison guards lived comfortably, making six-figure salaries through widely available overtime.

Cartel members were stymied. They felt hopeless enough to seek out a Yaqui Indian brujo, or medicine man, believed by some to possess extraordinary powers. Two young enforcers were sent to Sonora, a desolate Mexican territory that borders Arizona, to speak to a man named Jose Ruiz. Ruiz was a seventy-nine-year-old small landowner who was rumored to have occult powers. The old man was sitting with three other men on a bench outside a cantina in Aconchi, a small pueblo along the Sonora River. The narcoterrorists pulled up in a 5.0L V8 supercharged Range Rover, creating a dust cloud that danced in the air for five seconds, then blew into the faces of the old men. The narcos swaggered across the unpaved street toward the cantina.

"Which one of you is Jose?"

The old men were silent.

"Which one of you old-timers is Jose Ruiz?"

They were met by further silence. Jose had white hair and was thin, but lithe, agile, and solidly built. He studied the faces of the young men and decided they were in Aconchi for malevolent purposes. He contracted his abdomen and sighed.

"We're here to do business. We don't mean to disturb you. We've come from Sinaloa with a business proposition. We can make one of you rich." The narco pulled out a thick roll of American dollars. "This is just the retainer fee. We need a medicine man. Someone told us about Jose. We're not going to harm anyone."

"I'm Jose Ruiz."

"Are you what they call a 'brujo?'"

"What's a brujo?"

"Can we go inside?" the narco asked, nodding toward the cantina. "It must be a hundred degrees out here."

Jose sighed again, made brief eye contact with the other men, got up, and entered the cantina. The young narcos followed him and sat at a small unvarnished table beneath the only ceiling fan in the establishment. The cantina was empty.

"Look, old timer, let's get right down to business. A reliable source told us that you have mysterious powers. We'll offer you more money than you've ever seen in your life if you help us free someone being held against his will by the United States government."

The second narco interjected, "We need what ancient ones call a 'diablero.' Do you know of any?"

"What's a 'diablero?' I'm unfamiliar with that term."

"You know what, Pancho? I think you're playing possum. I think you know exactly what a diablero is. Let me refresh your memory. A diablero is someone who practices black sorcery—a shape-shifter, among other things. Someone who has the power to transform himself into an animal, maybe a coyote or a dog. Sound familiar? The Sonoran we tracked down in Mexico City couldn't remember anything either until we shot him in the shin. The bullets jostled his memory."

The young man pulled out an H&K P7M8, a single-stack 9mm handgun, and waved it at the old man.

3

"I shoot you in one of those skinny shins, your foot might fall off your leg. Is that what I gotta do to get you to talk?"

At that moment, the ceiling fan's motor began to whine, and when the young men looked up, a crow flew out the window of the cantina and disappeared. So had Jose Ruiz.

"Where the hell did he go?"

"What just happened?"

They searched the cantina and found no trace of Ruiz. One of the narcos pulled his cell phone from his jacket pocket.

"Arturo. Definitely some strange shit going on in Sonora. We came to the right place. Tell my uncle there's a guy here named Jose Ruiz who's a medicine man. Ask him to send someone down with a sniper rifle. We're going to have to shoot first, ask questions second. We're in a little backwards hole of a town called Aconchi, right on the river. I'm going to find a bar and cool off until they get here. Call me when they get close."

"Let's get back to the car and find somewhere air-conditioned to hang out for a few hours, drink some cold beverages," he suggested to the other narco.

"Do you believe that shit?"

"I wouldn't have believed it unless I saw it. Let's get out of this sweatbox."

The young men took two steps into the dusty street and the wolves attacked

4

them. Their throats were torn apart within seconds. Their bodies, still lying in the street in front of the cantina, were found a few hours later by the sniper.

Chapter Two

Two weeks later, the sister of the cartel leader went to Sonora. Her name was Ana. She drove a seven-year-old Ford Taurus and wore a plain pale yellow cotton shift dress that nearly touched the ground. She wore a dark, handwoven shawl called a rebozo. Long, thick braids gathered her straight white hair. Four old men were sitting on the bench outside of the cantina in the heat of the Sonoran morning. The woman spoke:

"I am very sorry if the two young men who passed through here a while ago caused a disturbance. Young people are sometimes disrespectful and don't appreciate the wisdom that comes with age. I apologize. I come here humbly with the hope that Jose Ruiz can assist me in some way, large or small."

The older men sat quietly listening.

"I have come to offer a gesture of goodwill because I believe that establishing a relationship between us can be mutually beneficial. I am asking to speak to Don Jose privately inside the cantina. If you are uncomfortable even for one moment, please tell me and I will leave and you will never hear from my family again. I promise that there will be no repercussions no matter what you decide. Will you please listen to my offer?"

Jose Ruiz, after a moment's reflection, got up and walked into the cantina. The other men remained on the bench. Jose Ruiz sat at the unvarnished table under the ceiling fan. The woman spoke:

"Don Jose. I'm here only to make what I hope is a benevolent gesture and I ask for nothing in return. You have a nephew, Francisco, who is being held without trial in Oaxaca, charged with sedition. He is being held unjustly. In Oaxaca, students and teachers are jailed for speaking out against the authorities with words that wouldn't raise an eyebrow in Mexico City. Even if the charges are dismissed, your nephew might remain in jail for a year.

"I have arranged for him to be freed tomorrow morning. I am leaving a bag on the floor that contains five hundred thousand pesos and a passport. It is for your nephew, no strings attached. A driver will pick up Francisco at the jail tomorrow morning and bring him to the Oaxaca airport with a ticket to General Morales Airport. Another driver will pick him up from that airport and bring him to you. He can use the money in any way he'd like. If he decides to return to Oaxaca, we have arranged for him to work in an artist's studio at the same salary he was earning teaching school. All charges against your nephew will be dropped by a magistrate on Monday.

"There are no strings attached at all to any of this, nor will there be any repercussions whatsoever if you decide you have no interest in helping us. But we have a rather urgent need of Sonoran sorcery."

Ruiz spoke for the first time. His dark neck and face were wrinkled, but his eyes were alert to every nuance and his body remarkably agile.

"What do you imagine this sorcery can do for you?"

"My brother is going to spend the remainder of his life in an American federal prison. Our lawyers keep insisting that we have no legal path to free him. With the glare of the news media and the politicians' rhetoric, we cannot bribe anyone to make his days comfortable. I know nothing about Sonoran sorcery but when the probable and possible are out of reach, we must expand our imagination and consider the improbable and impossible. We are hoping a diablero could create a possible path to my brother's freedom."

"Such things are very secretive, Señora. You are a mature woman and yet you've never heard of a diablero until very recently."

"We are desperate, Don Jose."

"I've never heard anyone admit to being a diablero."

"Why is that? If they're so powerful, why would they be concerned?"

"They are powerful but not immortal, by any means. If people knew someone was a diablero, they might conspire with others to kill him."

"Kill him?"

"Before the diablero killed them."

"Do diableros have a blood lust? Like vampires?"

"They have an amplified hunting instinct. If they see you as a threat, they will kill you."

"How do they travel?"

"I do not know the ways of a diablero. I do not understand their dark magic. People are naturally wary of them. One diablero can kill dozens, even hundreds of people. So people have killed them off. Only a few remain and they are most secretive."

"Are you a diablero, Don Jose?"

"I practice sorcery but I am not a diablero."

"Why aren't you wary of them?"

"I am as powerful as they are. There are many non-ordinary realities. Most people are afraid of the supernatural and choose not to see or notice. Not much could persuade me to leave Sonora, but I will explore your idea with others. I am looking forward to reuniting with my nephew. He is a warrior, if perhaps too much of an idealist for this cynical, corrupt world."

"If the diableros are willing to assist, will I be able to meet with them?"

"No. Perhaps you can give me an idea of what you are looking for?"

"My brother is being held for trial, supposedly housed at a high-security prison in Canaan, Pennsylvania. I believe that is a ruse. We have managed to acquire a small bit of information for a large sum of money. My brother may be secretly housed in an off-the-grid maximum security facility in Philadelphia. I need to set up a command post near this facility and direct an operation from there. Am I correct to believe that these diableros assume human shape for the majority of the time?"

"You could be standing next to one at the cantina and never notice. They appear fully human. The shape-shifting involves morphing into a powerful animal with great strength and agility and increased cunning and intuition. Some may have supernatural powers."

"But they remain mortal?"

"They are powerful spirits in human bodies and therefore mortal. Come back in two weeks and tell me the arrangements you've made near Philadelphia."

"I trust this will be a first step in establishing a path to my brother's freedom. Having powers like this at our disposal is heartening. I will provide all expense money and rent a house and hotel rooms near Philadelphia. I will buy a used car and register it to a deceased cousin. We will be fully operational when they arrive. I will fly to Philadelphia tomorrow. Our offer is one million American dollars to anyone who will help."

"I know two brothers and a cousin who are powerful hunters. Wolves. The last of the lineage. They have superhuman strength, reflexes, and balance. Bring the money in two weeks, one million dollars for each of them. Come humbly and come alone. Anyone who travels with you will not make it across the street. Anyone following you will measure their lifespan in minutes. No more talk for today. Thank you for your assistance with my nephew."

"Farewell, Don Jose."

Chapter Three

Gloucester City, New Jersey, has three water ice vendors, each with a distinct personality. Cabana was the first to set up shop, right smack on Broadway in the center of town. Cabana opened in 1991 and now seems every bit a part of the small town's historic district as the war monuments, churches, and banks. Cabana's customers are people running errands to the grocer's, the flower shops, or to Carr's Hardware, families from the west side of town, and children walking home from school. Cabana serves ice cream but attracts customers primarily with its sweet water ice. Cabana got in early to the "we make our own water ice" craze, as if there was something noble about making a product that contained fifty grams of sugar. Nevertheless, it is made with "real fruit" and customers are thrilled if they find a piece of lemon rind somewhere in the mixture. Nobody can argue that Cabana Water Ice isn't delicious. The place is clean and service is efficient. Cabana's owners are generous to the local school children, sponsor youth league athletic teams in town, and reward Little Leaguers after they win a big game. It is staffed by pretty girls from the local high school. If it had a theme song, it might be "Bus in These Streets" by Thundercat.

Twenty years after Cabana opened, a worthy competitor established itself on Johnson Boulevard, across from the Little League baseball and Ponytail softball ields. Here's The Scoop is an ice cream haven. A sign on the front window reads, "30 Flavors of Soft Serve." Their customers are children competing in day-long softball or baseball tournaments and families from the Highland Park section of Gloucester. Customers can socialize on benches along the front of their property. They sponsor youth league teams in Gloucester and are generous to town charities. Here's The Scoop is also staffed by pretty girls from the local high school. If it had a theme song, it might be the theme song from *Friends*.

A third icy confection establishment, Ottie's, opened in May 2017 at Bergen and Burlington Streets. Ottie's never pretends that anything it sells is freshly made. Its main attraction is an air-conditioned indoor dining area where customers can linger as long as they want at a half dozen tables spread throughout the room. Five Naugahyde spinning stools with checkerboard patterns circle the lip of the ordering counter. It is staffed morning, noon, and night by Ottie DiGiacomo, a quick-witted sixty-three-year-old, quick-tempered former high school football star. He opened the store hoping to supplement his Social Security income with a revenue stream the IRS didn't know about. He sells ice cream, water ice, soda, chips, freshly brewed coffee, candy, and anything else that fifteen-year-olds might impulsively buy. The kids like and respect him. A number of myths sprang up about Ottie that first summer the place was open: he had fought in the Vietnam War (he hadn't), he gained a thousand yards rushing as a halfback for the local high school his senior year (he had), his girlfriend was a stripper (he didn't have a girlfriend). He didn't sponsor any teams. The place was staffed only by Ottie. If the place had a theme song, it might be "See You Again" by Tyler, The Creator.

Ottie's is the center of another, more secretive scene in Gloucester. If you're a fifteen-year-old looking for weed, somebody at Ottie's knows somebody somewhere who has some. Weed is a golden thread that connects disparate social groups and cliques in small towns all over America. It creates an invisible brotherhood between the in-crowd, the outcasts, football linemen and marching band saxophone players, skateboarders, and aspiring rappers. The weed bond may be acknowledged only by a nod of heads in the cafeteria, a handshake that leaves teachers wondering how those guys knew each other, or a "hey" or "yo" shouted across a street or hallway. It's an underground brotherhood that recognizes no differences in race, religion, social class, family income, or skin color. And it didn't matter if you had ever physically smoked with another member of the marijuana underground—just the fact that you smoked cemented the bond. You were kindred spirits. In the '60s in Gloucester City, long hair, bell-bottom jeans, tie-dye shirts, miniskirts, fringed boots, head scarves, and leather vests were signals that you were open minded about weed. In 2017, it was hanging at Ottie's. It was a head shop without the bongs, glass pipes, and incense sticks. It's where Anthony Stanton became friends with Renee Sears.

14

Anthony Stanton was a fifteen-year-old wise guy who took the counter-argument in every discussion. A shock of black hair, rarely combed, and golden brown eyes accented his baby-faced innocence. The innocence was dispelled as soon as he spoke. Funny, bright, ornery, and handsome, interested only in NBA basketball, video games, and rap music, he figured people could take him or leave him. Plenty of people chose the latter. His dad left for parts unknown when he was ten. His mom thought he could do no wrong, but she was never around, having troubles of her own. Anthony was the smart kid who struggled to get a D. He never did an ounce of homework. "We do enough work in school," he pleaded. When his teachers pointed out that he hardly did any work in school, he'd tell them, "just sitting here listening to you is work." Arguing was a hobby. If you thought LeBron was the best player in the NBA, Anthony argued that Russell Westbrook was. If you thought Russell Westbrook was the best player in the NBA, he insisted that LeBron was.

Renee Sears was one of those kids who might need three paragraphs in the senior yearbook to describe her activities and contributions. At fifteen, she was already part of the student foundation of Gloucester High School. She participated in the drama presentation, the pep club, the school musical, the marching band, the color guard, the indoor percussion ensemble, and the Leadership Club. She sang the national anthem before the high school football games. She was the only girl in most of her STEM classes. She had piercing blue eyes, underscored by two islands of freckles. Her baby blonde hair had deepened over the years to a dark brown. Her parents were not-quite-reformed hippies, and the scent of marijuana had filled her home since she was in a playpen. Renee was as sincere as Anthony was cynical, and heads turned when people saw the two of them together.

They were not romantically involved. Anthony was involved with an older Catholic school girl who worked until eleven every night at her father's diner in Brooklawn. Renee, busy with music lessons and abundant extracurricular activities, had no time for romance. As a hobby, she made intricate birds out of origami paper and posted photos of them on Instagram. Anthony appreciated her innocence, and Renee was captivated by Anthony's guile. Ottie's closed at nine and Anthony and Renee usually stayed until closing then walked to Sherman Street and smoked in the living room of Anthony's house. After listening to some music, they walked to Johnson Boulevard and Here's The Scoop. They sat on the bench out front (the place closed at nine) until ten thirty. Then Anthony walked Renee to her house on Chambers Avenue and went home to take a shower and wait for his girlfriend to arrive.

Anthony and Renee would begin their sophomore year at Gloucester High in two weeks. On the evening of Friday, August 25, they sat together at Ottie's, drinking Orange Fanta sodas, scrolling through their Snapchat, Instagram, and

Twitter feeds, and glancing at Facebook. Anthony watched YouTube videos of NBA 2017 Las Vegas Summer League highlights over and over and over. Renee read comments people left about her origami birds on Instagram.

"Kevin Durant is so sick," Anthony said to no one in particular.

"Ott's getting ready to close," Renee reminded him.

"All right. Let's go get this night started right," he said.

The heat of summer had moderated and the evening temperatures felt invigorating. Renee sat on his couch when he went upstairs to "get the goods." He scrolled through the music on his phone and started streaming Kendrick Lamar's *Good Kid, M.A.A.D City* through a soundbar. They smoked, and Anthony turned up the volume when the song "Money Trees" came on.

"You know, this song is recorded over a Beach House track," Renee said.

"Who the heck's Beach House?"

"They're from Baltimore. A girl and a guy. They're great."

"They must be if Kendrick listens to them, but I never heard of them."

He adjusted the volume again and started dancing around his living room.

"JoJo, the Dancing Monkey," Renee teased. That prodded Anthony to slink and shake more demonstrably. "JoJo, the Dancing Monkey," Renee repeated.

When the album ended, Anthony and Renee headed to the benches in front of Here's The Scoop. They sat there every night discussing who were the best rappers, the possibility of life on other planets, the Kardashians' shenanigans, Anthony's umpteenth attempt to get Renee slightly interested in NBA basketball, what life must have been like for teenagers in the '60s, teachers at the high school, movies, comic books, the latest aggravations from their social media feeds, their hopes and dreams, their parents, why weed should be legalized, the meaning of Kendrick Lamar's songs, and their anxieties about a new school year that would begin in eleven days. They spent a lot of time staring across Johnson Boulevard at the skateboarders gliding on the blacktop parking lot near the youth softball fields. They were startled out of their mellow stupor that evening by movement that caught their attention in the twilight behind the Ponytail softball field.

"Did you see that?" Anthony asked. "It looked like a wolf just walked past the field!"

"There's another one!" Renee said. "But I don't think it's wolves. They look like big dogs."

"Dogs? Dogs don't move like that. They were wolves."

"I want to go see," Renee said. "Let's walk over."

"Hell, no. I am not getting eaten by a wolf. You go right ahead."

"And you're always saying I'm afraid of too many things! Let's just go see."

"Dude, I am legit afraid of wolves. Ain't apologizing for it. I'll walk you across the street and wait at the top of the hill for you. You're crazy."

They crossed Johnson Boulevard and one of the skateboarders, Trevor, walked over to them.

"You guys see those crazy looking dogs?" he asked.

"Dude, they ain't dogs, I guarantee it. They looked like skinny bears. Renee wants to go pet them. She's crazy."

"They were big. Look, there's another one! Definitely a wolf. Holy shit. Wolves right here in Gloucester," Trevor said.

"I want to get a closer look," Renee said. "I saw a red fox once out near the high school. They're more afraid of us than we are of them."

"No, dude, I'm definitely more afraid of them. Not about to go anywhere near a wolf," Anthony said.

Trevor spoke animatedly with the other skaters. Anthony retreated to the bench in front of Here's The Scoop. Renee walked toward the backstop behind home plate, where the security lights dimmed.

Anthony stood on a bench to get a better view of Renee. He couldn't see her in the darkness. The skaters began walking away toward Martin's Lake, a block away, hedging their bets in the dog/wolf debate.

"You guys see Renee?"

"Nah, man. Didn't see her. I think you're right. They were wolves. Dogs don't travel in packs like that. Those three animals were walking together."

"I can't believe I gotta go over there looking for Renee. Squirrels make me nervous, let alone wolves."

Anthony crossed Johnson and warily walked down the third base side of the softball fields into the dusky darkness. He scanned the fields on either side and saw nothing. He leaned on the industrialized protective wrap that covered the top of the outfield fence and looked for movement of some kind. Nothing.

"Renee!" he yelled. "Renee! Let's get out of here. C'mon. This ain't for me. My girlfriend's coming over. We gotta go."

No answer. Anthony fought every fear-filled impulse in his body and took step after step after step, slowly, surely, into the dark periphery of the sports complex, calling for Renee. After he walked past the playing fields and approached the building that housed the restrooms, the lighting dimmed. He forced himself to walk around the indoor batting cages at the complex's outer edge. It was pitch black. He squinted and tried to detect movement anywhere around the field, but the night was still.

"Renee! C'mon, dude. Stop playing. You win. I'm just as scared as you about stuff. Probably more scared. Like right now. Let's get out of here."

Anthony walked past the darkened snack stand where two hours ago kids begged their parents to buy them sugary bubblegum, red hot dollars, string licorice, and gummy bears. At eleven o'clock at night, it was a dark, dreary fortress of painted cinderblocks with a security shield over the front window. Anthony fought the urge to jog away and peered along the edge of the little hump bridge that led to Gloucester Heights. An opossum startled him as it ran along the water's edge.

"Renee," he yelled. "Sorry I said you were scared of too many things, all right? Come on out and stop playing."

He called her cell. After a series of rings, her voicemail came on, "Hi, this is Renee. Tell me something I don't already know." And then a beep.

"Renee. It's Anthony. What the hell. You owe me big time, dude. My balls are in my mouth walking around here in the dark looking for you. Call me as soon as you get this. Don't play any games, either."

He started walking home and called again, "Look, Renee. I hope you're just messing with me. I don't know what else I can do. Holy snap, was that scary. I'd go tell your parents but that might make it worse, so give me a break. I don't want to set off a panic. If I call 911 and you're messing with me, the cops are gonna be pissed. Plus, I got a joint in my wallet. I'm praying that you're only messing with me. I love you, Renee. In a way, anyway. Call me as soon as you get this, dude."

His girlfriend was waiting for him on his front steps.

Chapter Four

Anthony was awakened at 2 a.m. by a cacophony of door knocks, bell rings, and heavy footsteps on his front porch. He crawled over his still-sleeping girlfriend and walked to the front door, rubbing his eyes and shaking the remnants of a dream out of his head. He opened the door and saw three Gloucester cops with two police cars in the street behind them, lights flashing.

"Man, you guys ain't messing around. What's the matter?"

"Were you with Renee Sears tonight about ten thirty on Johnson Boulevard?"

"Yeah."

"How old are you?"

"Fifteen."

"Is your mom here?"

"No."

"Where is she?"

"Pretty sure that's none of your business."

"It is my business because I need both of you to come down to the station immediately, as in right now."

"Can I put on a t-shirt and get my sandals?"

"Hurry up. Call your mom and tell her she has to be at the station right away.

Anybody else in the house with you?"

"No."

Anthony's girlfriend stumbled out of his bedroom and walked up behind him.

"Tony, what's going on?"

"Thought you said nobody else was home," the cop said. "Can we come in and look through the house?"

"If you clap your hands the whole time so I know you're not taking anything."

"Go get your shirt and call your mom. We'll wait here."

Anthony put on a Golden State Warriors t-shirt and secured the straps on his sandals. He hugged his girlfriend and called his mom. She was at a friend's house in Bellmawr and left right away for the police station in Gloucester, a five-minute drive. When Anthony went back out onto the porch, there was one cop and one police car waiting.

"Ready, Freddie?" the cop asked.

"Guess I'm riding with you, huh? First time I ever rode in a police car."

"Have a feeling it won't be the last. You're a wiseass."

"I try my best."

When Anthony arrived, his mom was being briefed by the cops in the parking lot between the police station and the former Presbyterian Church.

"You know anything about all this?" she asked her son.

"Let's just go inside so I only have to say everything once. I didn't do anything so don't be edgy."

The police officer led them through a side door and into a conference room where a plainclothes detective stood talking with other officers. Anthony and his mother sat side by side. Anthony's mother signed papers granting the police permission to question her son. The detective introduced himself, reaching over the table to shake hands with Anthony's mother.

"I'm Detective O'Brien."

Anthony nodded hello.

"Anthony, how about we set some ground rules right off the bat. I'm going to treat you with total respect and I'm going to be completely honest. Think you can extend those same courtesies to me?"

"Sure."

"So no ball busting, no assuming the other guy is stupid. Is that good?"

"Sure."

"Tell me exactly what transpired between you and Renee Sears last night. I'm going to take some notes."

"Same thing that happened every night this summer, just about. We met at Ottie's. Dove into our phones, watched some stuff on YouTube, drank a couple of sodas. Left Ottie's around closing time, nine o'clock. Pretty much do that every

24

night."

"Ok. So nothing unusual about the first part of the evening. If I go around to Ottie's, he'll confirm all this, right?"

"Yes."

"What happened when you left?"

"We walked to my house. We might have smoked a little weed. We listened to Kendrick Lamar for about an hour. I was goofing around, showing off my Mick Jagger moves, dancing a little."

"Can you clarify something for me? Answer A: 'We smoked weed.' Answer B: 'We didn't smoke weed.'"

"Answer A, we smoked."

"Do you feel your judgment was impaired after smoking?"

"No more than it usually is. It calms me down, actually. Relieves my anxiety."

"Did Renee smoke weed also?"

"Awe, man, I really don't want to go there."

"It's significant, Anthony."

"Yes, she smoked."

"I'm asking you this next question with complete respect and I want you to answer it respectfully. Did you and Renee have any kind of physical relationship?"

"Not even once. Not one kiss ever, not even a hug. Being completely honest like you asked me. I have a girlfriend. Renee is just a close friend."

"Thank you. What did you do after listening to Kendrick Lamar?"

"We walked down Johnson Boulevard to Here's The Scoop. We sat on the benches and just watched the night go by."

"Can you recall about what time that was?"

"About ten fifteen."

"Then what happened?"

"We were sitting there talking about the solar eclipse and we saw these wolves walking behind the little kids' softball field. They turned toward the bigger field that Gloucester Catholic's team uses. Three wolves, all walking together. It was pretty crazy."

"Let's hit the pause button for a second, Anthony. Do you know how absurd that sounds?"

"Dude, it was absurd! You should have been there. The logo of the Minnesota Timberwolves came to life right on Johnson Boulevard, only there were three of them."

"And you don't think it had anything to do with the marijuana?"

"Dude, that's hilarious. We weren't hallucinating. We had a mild buzz. We saw three real wolves in Gloucester."

"Anthony, just for the record, buddy. I'm a lot older than you and I never heard of anyone seeing a wolf in Gloucester, or anywhere else in New Jersey for that matter. Not saying I don't believe you. I greatly appreciate that you've been honest. I'm taking you at your word. But I'm going to have to share this information with my boss, the police chief, and he's gonna laugh in my face."

"I'd probably laugh in your face, too, if I wasn't there to see it for myself. Renee wanted to go down and get a closer look at them, so we crossed Johnson and she went down the hill after them. I went back to the benches because I'm afraid of dogs, let alone wolves. Animals scare me. I don't trust anything you can't negotiate with."

"So Renee went off to pursue the wolves and you went to the bench. Then what happened?"

"I started getting nervous when I couldn't see her, so against my better judgment I crossed Johnson and went down the hill, walked across the railroad tracks, and looked for Renee."

"Anybody else around? Any cars stop? Anyone walking home who might have seen something? Anybody that we can talk to who may have seen a wolf on Johnson Boulevard?" He paused. "It's hard to even say that with a straight face, buddy."

"You know what? There were some dudes skateboarding along the blacktop behind the fields. They saw the wolves, too."

"How do you know that?"

"I walked past them when I went to look for Renee. They were hauling ass up to Martin's Lake because, like me, they weren't up for any wolf encounters."

"Do you know any of the skaters' names?"

"I know the one dude, Trevor."

"Trevor Morgan?"

"Yes."

"So if we go speak with Trevor, he'll substantiate that he saw Renee walking back to where it appeared three wolves were heading?"

"I guess. I hope. I don't see why he wouldn't."

"Okay, I'm going to ask one of the officers to go pick up Trevor. Just reminding you that it's three o'clock in the morning. Waking somebody up, waking his family up, well, his story better match yours, right?"

"I hope it matches. Don't see any reason he would lie."

"You sit here with your mom and I'll be back after we speak with Trevor."

An hour later, Detective O'Brien returned to the conference room. Both Anthony and his mom had fallen asleep with their heads laying on the table. O'Brien slapped the table.

"Hey, Anthony, time for school."

Anthony and his mom woke up, disoriented. O'Brien gave them a minute to get

28

their bearings.

"I spoke with Trevor and he confirms the details of your story. That doesn't necessarily clear you, but it gives credence to your story. Thank you for being honest. Trevor said he and his friends left and you kept looking for Renee. Is that right?"

"I kept looking for Renee. I must care about her more than I realized because I was more scared than I ever was in my life."

"You looked for her back by the batting cages?"

"I walked around every field. It was pitch dark behind the batting cages and I even looked there. I thought she might be hiding along that little creek bed in the back, near the hump bridge. I called her name over and over again. I called her cell and left a message. You can check that out if you want."

"Why didn't you call the police?"

"I wasn't completely sure she wasn't messing with me. I break her stones all the time because she always does her summer reading, always does her summer math packet, always goes to every practice she's supposed to be at. She's like a perfect person. I tell her she's scared of doing anything wrong. Thought she might enjoy watching me being scared, showing my true colors."

"But you went home after a certain while? Left your friend to fend for herself?"

"I tried to fight my selfishness and it worked. But only for a while. I reverted back to the self-centered dude I usually am. I'm sorry, but I did everything I could. I checked every inch of the place for her. Didn't realize I was capable of that. I must like her a lot because the usual me would have gone home right away. I stretched myself a lot. But was I perfect? No."

"Let's hope she's at a friend's house and calls her mom when she wakes up and it was a misunderstanding all the way around."

"But what about the wolves?"

"Anthony, I trust you. Some of the cops told me you'd be difficult but you were straight with me. However, there's nothing on Facebook, nothing on Twitter, nothing on Snapchat, nothing on Instagram, nothing anywhere on social media about wolves in Gloucester. We checked every site thoroughly. Know what that means in this day and age, buddy? It means it probably didn't happen. It might have been three particularly strange dogs, who knows. But if it ain't on social media, it probably ain't happened."

Chapter Five

Wolves may be the most efficient hunters on earth. They have the ability to adapt to any environment, and they thrive in a variety of climates and terrains. Once wolves arrive in an area, they focus on controlling a specific piece of land, which they mark as their territory. The size of the territory depends on the availability of prey and the geographic challenges there. In the wild, wolves primarily hunt moose, elk, caribou, and deer. Each of these animals has an acute sense of smell and hearing. These animals are capable of quick escapes. Wolves track their prey from downwind and remain out of sight until ready to attack. Wolves can run at speeds in excess of thirty-five miles per hour for short distances. They have great stamina and can run at slower speeds for much longer distances. Wolves will chase their prey for miles until the prey is exhausted. Wolves attack their prey at two preferred spots: the nose area or the rump. The prey usually dies of blood loss or shock. Each wolf is a formidable killer on its own and particularly lethal in a pack. Large prey, like bison, stand very little chance of surviving a wolf attack. Humans stand no chance.

The Highland Tavern on Orlando Avenue was packed on Saturday night with revelers celebrating the weekend and excited about the Mayweather-McGregor fight. August 26 had finally arrived after a summer of fight promotion that more closely resembled a professional wrestling feud than a legitimate sports rivalry. The majority of the crowd at the Highland hoped that the MMA titan would overcome daunting odds and defeat one of the greatest boxers of all time. The bout lasted ten rounds, made a fortune for the contestants, and was entertaining enough that most viewers were satisfied. Jack Devlin, a stevedore from Westville who worked on the docks in Gloucester unloading fruit for Del Monte, wasn't convinced.

"You guys are gullible," he told his friends after the bout. "That thing was choreographed from the opening bell until the ref pulled the plug. All that racial taunting and bluster over the summer was pure theatrics. A week from now, Mayweather and McGregor will be sharing a beer together at some private strip club in Miami, laughing at all the suckers that put up so much money to watch it. I'm glad I came here and watched it for free because it was hokey as all hell."

Devlin held a distinctly minority opinion among the four friends from the docks who sat in a booth beneath a Coors Lite clock.

"How do you figure it was choreographed?" his friends demanded to know. "Mayweather was beating the balls off him at the end."

"They hugged more than a group of college girls at their Homecoming game. I know Mayweather is a defensive boxer, but c'mon, some hungry Central American boxer would have beat McGregor in three rounds. Mayweather stretched it out for television. People will believe anything."

"You don't think Mayweather gave his all?"

"Yeah, in the ninth and tenth rounds. And I give McGregor a lot of respect for getting into the ring with him. But it was a scam."

"It was legit all the way! You're just a boxing fan who doesn't want to admit that the MMA is a better test of a man's toughness."

"I don't doubt that it is. I'm saying if you had a middleweight up-and-coming boxer, hungry and ambitious, no way does someone who never boxed before like Connor McGregor last ten rounds. They should have had Vince McMahon out there tonight. At least professional wrestling is winking at you."

"You're just an old crank, Devlin," his friend kidded.

"An old crank who's got to get the hell home. See you guys Monday."

Devlin threw forty bucks on the table to cover his tab for the night and headed to the rest room. He waved goodbye on the way out the side door and headed to the gravel lot behind the tavern. On the way to his car, a young man who worked in the refrigerated warehouse at Holt's called to him.

"Yo, Dev. Didn't see you in there. You don't usually hang out in Gloucester, do you?"

"Not normally, no, but I guess I was curious enough about the Mayweather fight to come here with Big Daddy and a few other guys."

"Listen, Dev. Will you talk to somebody from Del Monte and see if I can get on a crew that unloads the ships? The refrigerated warehouse is getting to me. I've got a cold six months a year. It's not natural. Can you talk with somebody? Seems like you know everybody down there. I can drive a forklift. I'm not afraid of enclosed spaces. I'd be perfect for unloading the boats."

"I'll try. Your work attendance good? If you've been missing time, you're not getting put on. Too many guys are looking for work. They want people who show up every day."

"My attendance is perfect. I'm there every day. It just ain't natural to work in a freezer. Anything you can do would be great."

"I'll put in a word for you. Now I gotta piss again. Don't ever get old. You have to piss every ten minutes. I gotta run back inside."

"Take a leak behind the trees back there, dude. Nobody's out here. It's dark as can be. You're a hundred feet from the street."

"Good idea. See you Monday."

"Thanks for anything you can do for me over there," he said, getting into his Dodge pickup.

Devlin walked back to behind the tree line, looking around to make sure no one was in sight. He hoped his wife had fallen asleep watching television so he could slip by her and pretend he had gotten home earlier. He pulled down the zipper of his jeans and hummed a riff from an old Chicago song, singing,

"25 or 6 to 4…"

Those were the final words of his life. He heard a sound in the underbrush and looked over his shoulder, expecting to see a squirrel or a raccoon. He quickly pulled up his zipper, then was attacked from the front by a wolf who bit into the nose and mouth area of his face. Two other wolves attacked from the rear, tearing his back and legs apart. Devlin was dead within seconds, his limbs left scattered in the darkness behind the tree line. These wolves had no interest in eating humans. They were only interested in killing them.

Chapter Six

In the final days of summer, the Gloucester City Police Department focused all its resources on the search for Renee Sears. Officers volunteered to work on their days off and after their assigned shifts were completed. Every hour that passed made it less likely they'd find Renee alive. Creek beds were raked. Wooded areas were searched. Yards and alleys were combed. Every inch of abandoned factories was scoured. But there were no signs of Renee.

Johnson Boulevard is less than a mile long and much of it is open public spaces: a bird sanctuary, Midget Football League complex, the town's Water Works, public basketball courts, Little League and Ponytail League fields, a small playground, and a jogging track. These areas were searched and searched again by the Camden County Prosecutor's Major Crimes Unit. Not a shred of evidence was discovered. Law enforcement officials were perplexed.

People in Gloucester fight like cousins on a two-week camping trip, but they always rally together to help anyone in need. A Town Watch group was organized to patrol Nicholson Road at night. A candlelight prayer vigil was held at Renee Sears' house on Chambers Avenue on Sunday evening. Neighbors dropped off meals to the police station and to the Sears family. Local ministers created a prayer chain and made solemn requests for Renee's safe return. By the end of the weekend, Renee's photo hung in just about every store window in the town.

On Sunday morning, Anthony Stanton was brought into the police station for further questioning by one of the officers who was on duty the night Renee disappeared. Anthony was willing to do whatever it took to ensure Renee's safety.

"Anthony, we now know that Renee was in great jeopardy the night you two saw the apparition down at the softball fields."

"What we saw were three wolves."

"Here's the thing, Anthony. No one who wasn't smoking a hallucinogenic plant saw any wolves that night. Just you and three skateboarders wearing Ozzy Osbourne t-shirts."

"And Renee."

"Taking your word for that, but she was smoking the same stuff, so she wouldn't be any more reliable than you."

"I told the detective the whole truth. Nothing but the truth."

"Well, then you probably don't care if I ask you a few questions about your statement that night?"

"Go ahead. I've got nothing to hide. You think anybody wants her found more than me?"

"You said you saw the wolves walking behind the smaller of the two softball fields. Would you say they came from the direction of the jogging track?"

"Yes, they were walking from that direction."

"So there's the first rub, Anthony. Unless these wolves were wearing moccasins, they'd have left footprints in the playground area. It's soft soil. We've had forensics experts from the Prosecutor's Office search the entire area for prints. They couldn't find any. That casts a lot of doubt about you and the Black Sabbath skate team seeing wolves."

"There's an easy explanation about why they didn't leave any tracks. They were walking on the blacktop the whole time."

The cop laughed. "C'mon, Anthony. Let's get real."

"Look, I don't know anything about wolves. I'm afraid of animals. They were walking along the blacktop."

"Maybe they called Uber. Maybe a driver dropped them off right at the parking lot," the cop said.

"Yeah, maybe."

"Or maybe you're full of shit and we ought to get down to the real nitty gritty about what happened to Renee that night."

"All right, dude."

"What'd you do with the body?"

"What body?"

"Renee's body."

"I never even touched Renee's body. Never kissed her. Never hugged her. Nothing. Zero."

"What did you do with the body, Anthony?"

"You know what, dude? Why don't you go rent a booth at one of those adult bookstores on Route 130. You can talk about this crap with the other perverts."

"Here's the thing, Anthony. We only have one suspect—you. You maintain that Renee was abducted by three wolves. And when she got abducted, you didn't call the cops, you didn't tell her parents, you went home and banged your girlfriend. At some point, we're going to find out the truth. You realize that, right? This charade about wolves isn't going to hold up. Talk with you soon, I'm sure. You're going to feel better once you tell somebody the truth."

"I am telling everybody the truth and I don't feel any better."

Anthony became a persona non grata in Gloucester. Older kids rolled down the car window and yelled "Wolfman" at him when they saw him on the street. Little kids made howling noises when he walked past. Everyone blamed him for corrupting Renee. He stopped at Ottie's on his way home from the police station.

"Wolfman Jack! What's up?"

"Ottie, my life couldn't suck any worse. I hate school, but I want school to start so I have something to distract me."

"Feeling unwelcome out on the street?"

"I was never real popular to begin with and now certain people think I put Renee at risk, or even hurt her myself, so just about everyone avoids me."

"I know you'd never hurt her. If I didn't know you had a girlfriend, I'd have thought you and Renee were in love. You guys were so at ease around each other."

"Wanna tell the cops that?"

"I already did, amigo."

"Really? When?"

"Naturally, they came in here asking a lot of questions yesterday. They're smarter than you think."

"Most of them are smart. One of them is whacked."

"Why don't you hang out with your girlfriend?"

"Ex-girlfriend. She's not allowed to talk to me. Her parents wigged out when they heard everything. They blocked me on her phone and she's not allowed on social media."

"Well, you're always welcome here, buddy. You know that," Ottie said.

"Thanks, dude. Maybe I'll see you tonight."

Anthony walked down Burlington Street, crossed Broadway, and headed to his house on Sherman. He hadn't seen his mom since the early Saturday morning interview at the police station. He walked up the steps and saw a piece of cardboard jammed into the edge of his front door. It read, "JoJo, the Dancing Monkey."

When Anthony turned it over, he saw three words:

Help me.

Renee

"Fuck no. No fucking way," Anthony said, crying and gagging on his words. He stumbled, spit in the street, and kicked over his neighbor's trash can.

"This can't be fucking happening. I love you, dude. I'll kill every fucking wolf in New Jersey."

Chapter Seven

The administrative staff of the Gloucester City Police Department had worked round-the-clock days since Renee disappeared. Sunday morning, Special Agent Mike Scher from the Philadelphia field office of the FBI called Gloucester police chief, Brian Moran. Scher requested a meeting at Honey's, a restaurant in the Northern Liberties section of Philadelphia, right over the Ben Franklin Bridge from Gloucester. He said it was urgent.

"I think I know what's going in in Gloucester City," he told Moran.

Chief Moran was perplexed but respectful and agreed to meet for lunch. He asked Detective O'Brien to accompany him. Honey's specialized in Black Fig French Toast and Squash Stuffed Chicken Breast, dishes you won't find on any menu in Gloucester. The restaurant had a private dining nook near the kitchen, reserved for professional athletes seeking privacy from fans wanting autographs. Philadelphia Phillies baseball players frequented the place since Chase Utley and his wife discovered it during his rookie season. FBI personnel in Philadelphia occasionally used the private booth for off-the-record interviews. Scher spotted the cops and walked over to greet them.

"Thanks for coming on such short notice," Scher said. "This is Agent Diego Gonzalez, a Class A Investigator from Mexico's Federal Ministerial Police. Agent

Gonzalez will provide some background information that might shed some light on some recent unusual activities in Gloucester City. I've been working with Gonzalez on a heightened security protocol for a federal prisoner being held nearby. We think that the recent events in Gloucester City are pertinent to our detail. I'll let Agent Gonzalez explain. Oh, and this meeting is off the record and I ask for assurances of complete confidentiality."

"Of course," Chief Moran replied.

"Positively," said O'Brien.

"The Federal Ministerial Police has a reliable informant in the Esteban Gracias drug cartel. I emphasize the word 'reliable' because he has provided us with accurate, valuable information so far and zero bullshit. When he says something's about to happen, it always happens. What I am going to tell you may sound baffling, but we are addressing the issue with extreme prudence, and I suggest that you do as well."

"You speak better English than Chief Moran," Detective O'Brien said.

"I went to college at UCLA," Gonzalez said.

"And you seem a lot smarter than Detective O'Brien, so I'm glad you're offering your assistance," Moran countered.

Gonzalez continued, "As you may be aware, Esteban Gracias has been deported to the United States to face charges that could result in many lifetimes of incarceration. His lieutenants have become frustrated because, unlike in my country, there is no chance your federal prison system can be compromised, no way to tunnel him out, no way to bribe prison guards, no way to influence the judiciary. Because of their growing desperation, the cartel has resorted to spending large sums of money on some extraordinary methods of freeing Gracias. In the Mexican state of Sonora, a form of sorcery is practiced by a small, very secretive coterie of Indians. A handful of these sorcerers, fewer than a half dozen, are referred to as 'diableros.' They practice sorcery that involves transmutating into animals, usually coyotes or wolves."

O'Brien asked, "Is a television crew going to charge in here and tell us we've been punked?"

Gonzalez smiled and continued, "Our informant tells us that three diableros have been hired to travel to the Philadelphia area to help Gracias break out of prison. I called Agent Scher and asked him to be watchful for any wolf or coyote sightings in this area."

"Wow," O'Brien said.

Gonzalez continued: "Gracias is said to be held in a federal prison in Canaan, Pennsylvania, until his trial begins in Brooklyn in two weeks. The Gracias cartel has concluded that their only chance to free him will be during his transfer to Brooklyn. They plan to spring him while he's en route from Pennsylvania to New

York. FBI tech people have been searching for police reports of wolves attacking humans, something wolves are not known to do. I understand that a young girl is missing in Gloucester."

"Correct."

"I realize this sounds fantastic and implausible. However, a month ago the cartel sent two narco gunmen up to Sonora to recruit a diablero. The narcos disrespected them somehow and were found with their necks severed. Their wounds were consistent with wolf bites. Their throats, esophaguses, and neck tendons were completely gone. Both narcos were armed and I presume could draw a gun out of their holster quicker than you can spit. Neither one had time to reach for his gun."

"Meaning?"

"Meaning the diableros are formidable adversaries, more demon than wolf. Anyone trying to kill one better do it from a distance."

"And you think that these diableros may have something to do with the young girl disappearing in Gloucester?"

"It's too much of a coincidence to explain in any other way. They were hired to come to Philly a week ago. Immediately afterwards, three wolves are spotted where a wolf hasn't been seen in a hundred years. Simultaneously, a young girl disappeared. Did you search for wolf tracks?"

"Yes, we had two forensics teams go over the entire area. We've been confounded. No tracks were found by either team."

"Diableros leave no tracks."

"Damn."

"They are ruthless and cunning," Gonzalez said.

"Should we be looking for humans, or wolves, or what?"

"They are shape-shifters. They present as humans the vast majority of the time," Gonzalez said.

"Why are they in Gloucester?"

"Because Gracias is being held nearby. I can't say where he's being held but it's not where the feds are telling the media," Scher said.

"Why don't the feds move him somewhere else?"

"That would be passing the problem down the line. The Gracias cartel will just move the operation to the new spot. This is a desperate, futile attempt to break him out of prison. It's a pipe dream. He's not getting broken out of prison. My superiors are insisting that we end this threat right here by killing the diableros. Another group of diableros won't be recruited. From what Gonzalez tells me, this may be end of the lineage."

Gonzalez resumed, "These ancient forms of sorcery have all but disappeared. Most people in Mexico would scoff at the very idea of a diablero. If you study

46

history, there have been many forms of magic that have died out. Vast accounts of magic appear in religious texts and history books. In medieval times, everyone believed in magic. Even today, many people believe in the paranormal—ghosts, extrasensory perception, UFOs, haunted houses, astrology, horoscopes."

"So Gloucester's stuck in this shit storm," O'Brien said.

"Sorry to say."

"Any suggestions?" Moran asked the FBI agent.

"I would put out a notification on social media that there has been a verified wolf sighting in Gloucester City. Say this is highly unusual and that the wolves should be considered dangerous and unpredictable. Emphasize that they are wild animals, far away from their natural habitat. Anyone who sees a wolf in Gloucester City or surrounding communities should immediately call 911. I'd suggest sending an internal memo to your county's police chiefs asking to be notified about any wolf sightings in other communities. I thought about issuing an official FBI report but that will attract notice from the national media and there'd be television cameras down at your softball fields, animal rights protesters picketing your police department, 'Save the Wolves' t-shirt vendors, half-drunk hunters, the whole human circus going full throttle," Scher said.

"Can you provide us with any resources?"

"Most definitely. Here's my cell number. We have forensics laboratories. We have satellite imagery we can call in. We have marksmen. What's the terrain like in Gloucester City?"

"Ninety-five percent concrete," the chief laughed.

"What about the missing girl? Any gut feelings?"

"My guess is that she's dead," Scher said.

"Do you also presume the girl is dead?" Moran asked Gonzalez.

"Yes, I do. I presume she's dead," Gonzalez said.

"You didn't touch your breakfast. Don't like Honey's?" Scher asked.

"Lost my appetite," Chief Moran said.

"What does the word 'diablero' mean?" asked Detective O'Brien, directing his question to Gonzalez.

"Devil."

Chapter Eight

Renee's disappearance drained some of the life force from Gloucester. Colors in trees and flowers seemed dialed back a few shades. The town was stunned. What happened on Johnson Boulevard seemed incomprehensible, scary, and mysterious. People's map of reality suddenly no longer matched the territory. Children didn't disappear in Gloucester. People helped each other. Neighbors looked out for each other.

Anthony walked into the big brick building on Monmouth Street that housed the police department, municipal courtroom, and traffic violations bureau. He went to the chief's secretary and respectfully asked to see Detective O'Brien. He was still crying, still staggered by the note on his door.

"He's out with the chief, honey. They had an important meeting in Philadelphia. Anything I can help you with?"

"No, thanks. I have to speak with the detective. I found something valuable."

"Well, then, he's going to want to speak with you. You can either leave me your number or you can go sit in the courtroom and wait. The courtroom's empty and the lights are off. Cool off for a while in the air-conditioning. Oops. Here they are now. I'll tell Detective O'Brien you're here."

Anthony studied a wall of somber photographs of former mayors and police chiefs. After a few minutes, Detective O'Brien came in.

"Anthony. Heard you want to see me. Something you forgot to tell the officer earlier this morning?"

"No, this just came up."

"C'mon, follow me," O'Brien said as they crossed a narrow hallway and entered an office.

"This is the police chief, Chief Moran. Mind if he hears it?"

"Well, it's kind of private."

"He'll hear it anyway, Anthony. He's my boss. Do you want to go to the conference room so nobody else is around? We can do that."

The three of them walked to the private interview room. Detective O'Brien and the chief sat at the table. Anthony walked in short circles.

"When I went home today after getting interviewed by that cop, I found this wedged in my front door."

He handed the piece of cardboard to the detective.

"'JoJo, the Dancing Monkey.' What the heck's that mean?"

"Renee and I went to my house after Ottie's closed Friday night."

"Right, you told me. You and Renee listened to music?"

"Yes. When we were listening to this one song, I started goofing around and dancing and Renee said, 'JoJo, the Dancing Monkey.' She said it twice. I don't know how she came up with it. But no one else has ever said those words to me ever, not once. The cardboard had to come from Renee."

"You think she put it in your door?"

"Turn it over."

"Hmmm. Take a look at this," O'Brien said and handed it to the chief.

"'Help me. Renee.'"

"This was wedged in your door this morning?"

Anthony started shaking and crying, got down on his knees, and put his head on the floor.

"Think it's legit?" the chief asked O'Brien.

"Yeah."

"Think she's still alive?"

"Yep."

Anthony got up off the floor and pulled off his t-shirt to dry his eyes and nose.

"Tie me to a fucking tree down at the ballfields with pieces of steak on my body. Draw those fuckers out and have somebody shoot them."

"All right, buddy. Calm down."

The three of them sat, two veteran law enforcers and a fifteen-year-old, bare chested and trying to calm his breathing.

"You cannot mention this note to anyone. Hear me, Anthony? Nobody. Not your mom, not Ottie, not your friends."

"That part's easy. I don't have any friends anymore."

"Maybe you should try not using the F word in every sentence," the chief said. "You seem likable enough to me."

"Can I go tell Renee's parents?"

"No," O'Brien said. "We'll put our heads together, consult some experts, figure out how to move forward without jeopardizing Renee's safety."

"There's experts in wolf kidnappings?"

"Maybe. And that's another thing you can work on. Stop being a wiseass. You work on that, and we'll work on figuring out what the heck's going on. Deal?"

"Yeah."

"Call us immediately if anything else happens. I'm going to tell the office staff that if you call or come in, they can interrupt whatever I'm doing."

"Thanks."

"This is good news, buddy. Be smart. Not a word to anybody."

"I hear you. Just find Renee."

Chapter Nine

Elena Goodins was Gloucester's unofficial gossip columnist on Facebook. A cheerleader at Gloucester High during the 1980s, Elena had grown meaner every year. Twice married ("I'm never doing that again," she assured people), living on Broadway in a big old house right across from the post office (better to see who was going in and out of Gloucester Liquors), and out of work while receiving disability checks after developing "back issues" while working at McGroarty's, a small news agency that sold hoagies, milk, and wrestling magazines, Elena provided the dirt that started a dozen small town scandals. If you were laid off because your company was relocating down South, she had no interest. But if you were terminated because of drinking or drug issues, Elena blew so hard on the gossip horn there wasn't a person in Gloucester who didn't know about it before dinner. Elena revealed her half-truths in cryptic comments on Facebook, soliciting a demand for more info from other tongue waggers. For example, Elena would pronounce:

"No wonder why the ambulance takes so long to respond. Bunch of drunks…"

That post would set off a deluge of "What happened?????" and "That's terrible!!!!!" responses, followed by anecdotes about the time the local ambulance went to the wrong house or went down a one-way street taking someone's uncle to dialysis. After an hour of feverish responses, Elena would issue another edict, having reflected on the confusion of the masses:

"Maybe somebody should go see a lawyer."

Her post would set off a frenzy of self-recrimination for not realizing how serious the situation was sooner (Aunt Connie's stroke!), fueled criticism of town officials, and cast further aspersions on the local EMTs. Elena Goodins was always the first with the worst. If a cop was seen flirting with a waitress at the local diner, Elena spread the word ("Boys in blue better remember they have wedding bands on their fingers"). If a young coach at the high school was under suspicion for being improperly close to a student athlete, Elena sounded the sentinel ("I'm sorry, but young guys should not be coaching teenage girls. Sorry, not sorry."). She knew who was in rehab, who was suspended from the team, who was going to marriage counseling, why the local priest was transferred, who had been diagnosed with cancer, who got a DUI, why any random guy had his hand in a cast, whose kids had head lice, who was flirting with whom at Wawa, which companies were closing, and whose marriage was in peril. No one in Gloucester was less popular on the street, but she had two thousand friends on social media, many of whom had designated her a "See First" status on Facebook. On Monday, August 28, right after she finished a lunch of four Krispy Kreme Apple Fritters, Elena shocked the city:

"Dead body at the Highland."

The ensuing hysteria of "Wtf!" "We're moving!!" and "This town's getting more like Camden every day" set a personal response record for Elena (she kept a count of "Likes," "Shares," and replies in a notebook she kept on her computer desk).

Jack Devlin's wife, Joyce, had extended her arm across the bed Sunday morning and reached to feel her husband, assuming he had come home from watching the fight. Jack's side of the bed was cool and empty. It did not alarm her. Jack frequently overdid the drinking when he went out with his friends and knew better than to get behind the wheel afterwards. It was weird he didn't call, she thought, but he probably ended up sleeping on a friend's couch. He earned these nights, she felt. Jack drove a forklift into the bowels of a ship five days a week, carrying crates of bananas and grapes through a labyrinth of narrow ramps along the dark confines of a cargo container ship that had traveled thousands of miles from Chile to Gloucester. So what if he got shit-faced every couple of months and didn't make it home to Westville? He was not a womanizer, gambler, or drug user. Jack was a man of few needs. He loved his wife, supported his adult children, and adored his grandkids. As an added bonus, Joyce knew that Jack would green light a trip to the Coach outlet as a make-up gesture for not coming home.

But when Jack hadn't called by noon Sunday, Joyce knew there was trouble. Jack didn't use his cell phone enough for the battery to run down. She paced the floor of their bungalow on River Drive for an hour and then called the Westville police. The Westville police sergeant respected the Devlins and promised to put out a missing persons report if Jack didn't show up by dinner.

Meanwhile, the owner of the Highland Tavern noticed a car in his lot when he came into work on Sunday, but that wasn't unusual in the age of Uber and people's reluctance to drive after drinking. In the past, having a car left in the lot overnight may have raised a concern, but nowadays it was commonplace for someone who had a few too many drinks to find a ride home. Probably still sleeping off last night, he thought. They'd be back later for their car.

Joyce went to the Westville Police Station on Crown Point Road at 6 p.m. Jack Devlin was not at "high risk" (children, the mentally impaired, long-term missing persons) according to New Jersey missing persons protocols, but the police were supportive and sent out a bulletin to surrounding communities. They emailed the Gloucester PD because Joyce thought her husband might have watched the fight in Gloucester. Besides a six-man brawl outside of Solly's, there were no unusual activities reported in Gloucester after the boxing match.

When the owner of the Highland came to work on Monday morning and spotted

Devlin's car still sitting in his back lot, he called the police to get it towed. The county police dispatcher looked up the license plate, remembered that Jack Devlin had been reported missing out of Westville, and called the Gloucester Police Department with the information. A Gloucester police officer was dispatched to the Highland, expecting to do nothing more than call a tow truck. She looked around to see if anything looked amiss and discovered a human limb nestled inside a size 12 Timberland Classics work boot; a halo of flies obscured the sunlight beaming through the trees. She put her head down and retched, then called her sergeant after she regained her composure. By noon, the parking lot at the Highland Tavern was declared a crime scene, other body parts were discovered, forensics detectives from the Major Crimes Unit were summoned, and Police Chief Brian Moran had called Mike Scher. Moran told Scher about the dead body and his presumption that it was a wolf attack.

"Your primary problem is how to stop future attacks with limited manpower. A second problem will be containing the hysteria once word gets out. You want to meet for lunch? Gonzalez and I can drive over to Gloucester," Scher said.

"There's a place called Dolson's Tavern on the Edge. Mapquest it, it's on Jersey Avenue. They have a second-floor deck we can use and have privacy. Can you get here right away? I have to release a statement soon," Moran replied.

"Meet you at Dolson's in an hour," Scher said.

Chapter Ten

For families with school children, the last days of summer are bittersweet. Kids trade late-night video games, sleepy mornings, swimming, fishing, summer jobs, and bare feet for enforced bed times, early morning wake ups, organized sports, homework, and seeing friends they didn't get to see over the summer. Parents trade free babysitting, moving at a relaxed pace, easy meals on the grill, and enjoying a vacation of their own for being a drill sergeant every morning, managing car pools, employing child care, packing lunches, and nagging kids about homework. Everyone starts appreciating weekends again.

The anticipation of the new school year provided a distraction that briefly muted fascination with Renee's disappearance. The search for backpacks, sneakers, notebooks, and folders became a primary family focus. Teenagers became excited about the prospects of a new school year. All eyes were on the football team, beginning the season before Labor Day for the first time in history. Field hockey, cross country, and soccer teams practiced six days a week and opened their scholastic sports season the day after Labor Day. Marching band and color guard members rehearsed. The dance team and cheerleaders perfected new routines. The effort, excitement, and weariness of daily practices in the August sun dampened discussions about Renee. But when the high school opened on

September 6, and Renee's beatific presence wasn't felt in the classrooms and hallways, people discussed little else.

It was against that backdrop that police chief Brian Moran walked up the steps of Tavern on the Edge and asked Rich Dolson if he could talk to a federal law enforcement guy (trying to avoid the phrase "FBI") on the top deck of the restaurant.

"Sure thing, Brian. Take as long as you want," Dolson said.

Moran greeted Scher and led him upstairs.

"I'll send a server up in five minutes," Dolson said.

Moran and Scher went out onto the deck, sliding the door closed behind them.

"We found a body this morning in a small wooded area behind a local tavern. Middle-aged White male. Torn to pieces. Front of the face bitten off. No witnesses. County Prosecutor's staff is sifting through the crime scene. O'Brien's out there. I'll have to say something to the reporters once his family is notified. Going to be front page news for a while. Any suggestions?"

"No suggestions that are going to make it less unpleasant."

"The entire thing is too fantastic. I'm just going to stick with the facts and not bring up any of the diablero stuff. Not going to mention anything about the cartel leader."

"They ain't gonna learn what they don't wanna know, and people do not want to know about evil spirits running loose. That's for darn sure."

"I'll say it was an animal attack and we're waiting to see what the Prosecutor's Office concludes," Moran said.

"I'll schedule a meeting with the Prosecutor and bring them into the loop. We should go on the offensive against the diableros. If Mexican villagers have nearly wiped them out, I like our chances. From this point forward, we should be aggressive. The only way to make them disappear is to make them disappear," Scher said.

Moran looked at his phone.

"It's O'Brien," he said, and spoke to the detective. Scher headed for a rest room. When he returned, Moran said, "The Prosecutor's forensics staff says the wounds are consistent with an animal attack. They'll want to run tissue tests before committing any further. They're operating within a normal evidence paradigm, so the sooner you can brief them, the better. Their offices are five minutes from here."

Scher called and asked his clerk to schedule a meeting that afternoon with the Camden County Prosecutor.

"Tell them it's an emergency and that it's related to the attack in Gloucester City."

"If I say it was a wolf attack, any half-bright reporter is going to counter with: A) There aren't any wolves in New Jersey, and B) Wolves don't attack for sport," Moran said.

Scher shook his head. "If they start questioning you, say you're waiting for tissue and toxicology reports and don't want to speculate. You're smart saying it's a wolf. Maybe somebody else thought they saw a wolf on Friday but is hesitant to say."

Chief Moran held a press conference Monday afternoon at 5 p.m. in the City Council chambers on Monmouth Street. The conference was covered by three young interns from *The Philadelphia Inquirer*, South Jersey's *Courier Post*, and KYW Newsradio. They listened respectfully as Moran spoke:

"Three wolves were spotted in Gloucester City on Friday evening, August 25, by a group of high school students at approximately ten p.m. A fifteen-year-old girl pursued the wolves to get a better look at them and has disappeared. The area along Johnson Boulevard where the wolves were spotted has been searched exhaustively by police officers and forensics scientists. No trace of the missing girl has been found. On Monday morning, the body of a fifty-one-year-old White male was discovered in a wooded area behind a tavern on Orlando Avenue. Forensic scientists are examining tissue samples of the body, and no definitive explanation can be offered at this point. Preliminary indications suggest the wounds are consistent with a wolf attack. I realize that wolves are not known to exist in New Jersey, especially not in a predominantly urban setting like Gloucester City, but evidence uncovered so far points in that direction. Most naturalists insist that wolves do not attack for sport, so the circumstances in these cases are unusual and improbable. However, it is the only direction that real-life, real-time evidence is pointing toward. The Federal Bureau of Investigation, the Camden County Sheriff's Department, and the County Prosecutor's Office are assisting with the probe. Any citizen who sees anything unusual, please contact the police immediately. Do not confront the wolves without police assistance. Police have been working extra shifts since the young girl disappeared and will continue to work voluntary overtime. We will hold a press conference here tomorrow at five o'clock. I'm going to decline any questions now because I've provided all of the genuine information available and I prefer not to speculate."

The reporters thanked him, gathered their equipment, and left. The press conference ended at five fifteen. Five hours later, reporters from all major Philadelphia area news media were encamped in the parking lot of Gloucester Catholic High School's annex building, catercorner from the police station. ABC, NBC, CBS, and FOX affiliates arrived. *The Philadelphia Inquirer* dispatched a photographer and two reporters to Johnson Boulevard, seeking people's reactions and digging for information. By daybreak, reporters were huddled on the corner of

Brown Street and Chambers Avenue, hoping to interview the Sears family.

No wolves were spotted on Monday. Police officers spent the day working on car burglaries, administering Naloxone to unconscious opiate users, and serving warrants. The Philadelphia FOX affiliate headlined their ten o'clock news intro with "FOX looks for wolves in Gloucester City." The New Jersey State Police offered Chief Moran immediate access to their Special Weapons and Tactics Team and their Technical Response Bureau. People walked the streets deep into the night, trying to catch a glimpse of the wolves. Monday night was quiet. Tuesday would be a different story.

Chapter Eleven

Tuesday began and ended with a dead body. O'Brien met the cops from the night shift at Dunkin' Donuts every morning to get a feel for what happened overnight. He was looking for the story behind the story, the details left off the official police report. He picked up the tab for everybody each morning, hoping that most of the shift would show up and share their insights with him. The cops talked also about the Phillies and the Eagles and their families and shared a few laughs each morning. On Tuesday morning, O'Brien's cell phone buzzed. He looked at the screen and cringed.

"Why the hell did I ever give John Caseban my cell number?"

"Didn't you guys date in high school?"

"If I don't answer it, he'll call back in five minutes...and every five minutes until I do answer," he said. He shook his head and answered the call.

"Yo, dude. Can't wait to hear what you need to talk with me about at six thirty in the morning," O'Brien said.

"If I didn't think that you're sitting around with the other lazy asses at Dunkin' Donuts, I wouldn't bother you this early."

"As a matter of fact, I'm changing my kid's diaper before I go in to work to wrestle with the filth of human society. So this better be good."

"You know those three wolves the high school kids saw down on Johnson Boulevard?"

"Yeah."

"Well, there's gonna be one less wolf in the wolf pack this morning, hombre, because I just put a hole in one of them with my Mossberg Patriot."

"Don't be messing with me, John," O'Brien said, walking outside to the parking lot.

"True story, dude. But there's one sticky complication, which is why I called you so early on your cell. Can you spare ten minutes and meet me on Park Avenue near that old grammar school?"

"Highland Park School? The one that's closed?" O'Brien asked.

"That's the one, hombre. Come alone. Like I said, there's one less wolf but it's never smooth sailing when it comes to a John Caseban operation. You know that."

"Coming right out."

O'Brien walked back into Dunkin, grabbed his coffee, and told the cops to go get some sleep. He drove his unmarked car to the shuttered grammar school and looked for John Caseban. Someone whistled from a wooded area across Park Avenue and he spotted Caseban, dressed in blue Army/Navy store camos.

"What happened, John?"

"Well, I had my own little wolf patrol operation, considering I'm out of work and not busy doing anything else. I was driving around in my truck all night, searching and looking. I turned off Market onto Weston. When I turned down Gaskill, I saw one of the bastards creeping into the woods. I parked the truck and crept down here slow as shit. I know how to hunt. If you could get paid for hunting, I wouldn't be out of work."

"How many wolves did you see?"

"Let me continue, my man. I saw one wolf. Followed him into these woods, maybe a hundred feet behind him. The wolf had his back to me and was pawing at the ground like he was preparing a place to lie down. The Mossberg's got a great scope. Took my time and gently pulled the trigger. Blew a hole in him you could watch television through."

"Where's the body?"

"That's where things get strange. I reloaded right away because I thought the other wolves might be around. The carcass was laying on the ground in front of the tree. It was cloudy and there wasn't much light. My senses were on five-alarm alert, dude. I tiptoed over, hoping to get a nice selfie of me and the big bad wolf, when my luck turned bad. It wasn't a wolf carcass laying there, it was a human. Deader than dead, but a human. Big hole in his back. I'm thinking, what the hell did I just do?"

"Where's the body, John?"

66

"It gets weirder, dude. I start panicking, right. Like, I just friggin' killed somebody! Pacing around trying to figure out what to do. I look back at the tree, thinking maybe I could cover the body with some leaves or fallen tree limb—but there wasn't a body. There was nothing but a big pool of red grease."

"What? Show me."

Caseban led O'Brien through a thicket of vines, fallen tree branches, weeds, and discarded trash, finally coming to a clearing where the men could walk in stride instead of stepping through overgrown vegetation. At the foot of a twenty-foot oak was puddle of red grease with purple and orange swirls. A piece of straw floated on the right edge.

"John, listen to me. This is a crime scene from here on in. You might be declared a hero in a day or two. But DO NOT post anything on social media or tell anybody about any of this, because if the forensics people say this contains human DNA, and it might, you'd be in major trouble and nobody is going to believe that a wolf morphed into a person, got me?"

"I feel you. Thanks, dude. Thought I could trust you."

"Not one word at all to anybody, John, until I call you and tell you you're cleared, understand?"

"Totally."

"All right, get out of here. I have to call in this in."

O'Brien called the chief.

"Hey, you know that kook, John Caseban?"

"Yeah. What about him?"

"He killed one of the diableros. In that wooded area between Gaskill and Park. I believe him. I'm out here now. Really crazy. He said the wolf morphed into a human and then disintegrated into a puddle of grease."

"What?"

"Chief, it's like Gonzalez said, there's some crazy voodoo going on."

"One down, two to go. Did you tell him not to say anything? He's a big mouth."

"I scared him, pretty sure. Don't think he will. I'll tape off this area of the woods. We need a forensics team. Did Scher ever tell the Prosecutor's Office?"

"He met with them yesterday."

"They should come collect this grease or blood or whatever the hell it is. And it's starting to rain. It's getting blocked by the tree canopy now but if it starts raining harder, it's going to affect the crime scene."

"They'll come right out," the chief said. "I'll send a couple of cops out to help secure the scene."

Anthony walked into Ottie's, feeling optimistic for the first time since Friday.

"Anthony, the wheel of life is always in spin. First you were a ball-busting, unmotivated pain in the ass. Then you became a villain for a couple of days. Now you're a hero. Guess you were right about those wolves," Ottie said.

"Wish they'd find Renee."

"No clues at all yet?"

"I heard some dude shot one of the wolves."

"Somebody shot one?"

"Yeah, people were sharing the guy's picture on Facebook. Guy named John Caseban. He took a selfie standing out on Gaskill Avenue holding this big Mossberg Patriot rifle. He said the wolf charged him and he blew the wolf's head off. Said he'll get the other two wolves tonight."

"And it's legit?"

"People keep sharing it. He looks kinda unstable. But apparently he did kill a wolf, and that's good," Anthony said.

"I'll believe it if the police confirm it," Ottie said. "People are saying all kinds of stuff about the wolves. You know that old drunk, Chick Austen, who stands in front of the bank on Monmouth Street asking everybody for a dollar?"

"Yeah."

"I went to the bank this morning and he told me he was sleeping in one of the dugouts at Gloucester High's baseball fields and he saw two wolves walk past the dugout. He looked to see where they were going, and he says they got into the back of a black van. Said a lady closed the door behind them and drove away."

"Huh?"

"That guy's brain is marinated," Ottie laughed.

"I'm going to walk around town to see if I hear anything about Renee."

"Be careful, buddy. That wheel's always in spin, right? Nobody's on top for too long."

Chapter Twelve

In the twenty-four hours since Chief Moran first walked into Gloucester's makeshift press room, the story of the wolves had become much more frenzied and fantastic. Yesterday's interns were replaced by skilled veterans from the Philadelphia media. As the stature of the story grew, the stature of the reporters grew. Something strange was happening in Gloucester City and smart people could sense it. Something far out of the ordinary. Chief Moran nervously took the podium.

"I'll begin with the factual evidence: A fifteen-year-old girl, Renee Sears, disappeared Friday night under mysterious circumstances. Multiple searches of the surrounding area by forensic scientists have yielded no clues. A fifty-one-year-old male, John Devlin, of Westville, suffered fatal wounds consistent with a wolf attack. We do not have conclusive tissue and toxicology reports yet, so I will not be speculating any further on Mr. Devlin's case. Additionally, a local hunter saw a wolf in a wooded area across Route 130 early this morning and shot and killed it. Forensic scientists at the FBI field office in Philadelphia are examining the remains of the carcass. We will await a definitive assessment of the animal's genetic makeup. I am going to turn the remainder of the conference over to Special Agent Mike Scher of the FBI."

"Chief Moran has presented the factual evidence. I will be happy to answer any questions, but I'm not going to posit anything that doesn't have an evidentiary grounding," Scher said.

A reporter in a polka dot frock asked, "Why is the FBI involved in a case that seems more like a matter of wildlife encroaching on urban landscapes?"

"The wolves may have crossed state lines, so it's become a federal matter," Scher joked. A few reporters grinned, and he continued. "I contacted Chief Moran after reading the police report detailing the disappearance of the young girl and the concurrent wolf sightings in Gloucester City. I offered our forensic lab to his police department. This is an unusual event, and certain aspects of it may be contrary to what I call 'police science.' I was hoping to help in some small way, but the Gloucester Police have handled everything perfectly. I've been a fifth wheel."

A reporter interrupted: "A number of things do not make logical sense here, sir. Wolves do not live in New Jersey. Wolves don't attack what they don't eat. Wolves hunt in packs and yet the hunter claims on his social media that there was only one wolf in the woods. You claim these are wolf attacks, but I don't see any evidence of that."

"Science takes time. Perhaps we're dealing with a hybrid of a wolf and another animal. Any evidence that has been collected may be puzzling scientists because

72

there's a chance no existing DNA template can identify what we're seeing."

Television camera operators strained to get a better angle. Reporters scribbled furiously. Chief Moran caught Scher's attention and held up one finger.

"Ok, one more question for this evening and then we'll see you tomorrow at five o'clock."

"With all due respect, I have a feeling you're not being completely forthright, Agent Scher," said a reporter with salt-and-pepper hair, wearing a J. Crew sport coat over Fidelity jeans.

Scher paused. "I've had the same questions as you. What are wolves doing in New Jersey? Why are they attacking humans? Why can't we find even a small piece of evidence that will assist us in the disappearance of the young girl? These questions bother me, and I can understand why they bother you. However, many of the energies that drive our lives remain unseen. Magnetic fields, gravity, the electrical currents that are powering your cameras, thoughts, moods, morals, passions. They are all invisible and can't be quantified or explained. But that doesn't mean they don't exist. They do exist. They energize the world. We are searching for forces that are energizing these strange occurrences. The energies are invisible at this point. We humbly acknowledge that the invisible world often governs the visible. We are seeking to understand which invisible energies are driving these occurrences in Gloucester City. Thank you for your interest."

Moran, O'Brien, and Scher returned to the privacy of Moran's office.

"You're a pro, dude. Sounded like Carl Sagan up there. I felt like I was watching PBS," O'Brien said.

"And you immediately wanted to switch the channel?" Scher joked.

"No, I was enjoying it. Those reporters are a bunch of wolves," O'Brien said.

"Well, they were out in the rain all day. Felt like Seattle around here. Doesn't do much for anyone's mood. The only excitement was that crazy guy shooting the wolf."

John Caseban was riding in his pickup listening to Ted Nugent and dreaming of the next kill. "Finally got my break," Caseban told himself. "I get another wolf, I'm going on YouTube. This is national news."

Caseban explored the Johnson Boulevard area, where the wolves were first sighted. He began at the so-called bird sanctuary at Johnson and Morris. What a joke, he thought. A bird sanctuary for sparrows and robins. He walked behind the woods that surrounded the swim club and couldn't shake the feeling that someone was watching him. Every cop's a tough guy now that the reporters are here, he thought. Finally found something to get them off their lazy asses. Probably spying on me.

74

He looked around a few times, half expecting to see O'Brien.

Watch how a man hunts, sucker. Most of you guys have never fired your pistol outside the shooting range.

Forty-five minutes later, drug pilgrims riding their twenty-inch bicycles onto Collings Road noticed what appeared to be a human arm sticking out of the tall weeds beneath the Walt Whitman Bridge. Police were dispatched to the area and discovered a human body, completely torn apart, with tattered blue camos covering parts of the back and legs and a Mossberg Patriot rifle still gripped by one of the hands.

Chapter Thirteen

Facebook conspiracy theorists went into overdrive concerning the wolves of Gloucester. Some cited climate change. Others claimed that the never-ending expansion of housing developments onto woods and farmlands disrupted animal habitats. A church in Alabama speculated that the wolves were an apocalyptic punishment because Gloucester High permitted a lesbian couple to attend the prom last spring. Republicans blamed Democrats (too much aid to failing inner cities left little for wildlife preservation). Democrats blamed Republicans (the shale industry in Pennsylvania had disrupted the fragile ecosystem).

Police worked through the night scrubbing the area where John Caseban met his death.

Chief Moran had worked the past twenty hours and was less than thrilled to see his ne'er-do-well cousin, Nick Sheddon, walk into his office. Nick saw him at the start of every school year for a "loan" to get backpacks and school supplies for his kids. Nick worked part-time cleaning business offices and picked up an occasional shift at the high school as a substitute maintenance worker.

"Cut right to the chase, Nicky. Who needs what, and how much? Really crazy around here right now," the chief said, pulling out his wallet.

"No, it's not that. Well, okay, if you've got a hundred you can spare, I'll take it.

Much appreciated. But that's not why I'm here. Can I close the door?"

"It's gotta be quick, Nick. I'm dealing with some crazy stuff."

"Because of those wolves?"

"Yeah, because of those wolves."

"That's why I'm here to see you."

"What's up? You friends with John Caseban?"

"Brian, I saw the craziest thing. I was working maintenance, doing the midnight shift at the high school last night. I was having a smoke during my break, sitting on the steps of C-wing about three o'clock this morning. Cleaning C-wing's a cinch now that the junior high moved out."

"Nick, spare me the details. What did you see?" the chief said.

"I saw the wolves."

"Where?"

"When I was sitting on the C-wing steps I saw two wolves slinking along the fence separating the school property from the businesses on Route 130."

"What'd you do?"

"Opened the door to C-wing and jumped inside before they noticed me."

"That it?"

"I looked out the windows to see where the wolves went. This part is nuts. They went under the fence between the car wash and the high school and I swear on my life, they got into a black van with some older Mexican lady behind the wheel. She had the back door open and closed it once they got in."

"You have anything to drink before work?"

"Dude, I ain't drank a single drop since the end of July. Jen said she was gonna leave my sorry ass because I fell asleep minding the kids while she was at work. I was sober as a nun, Brian. I know what I saw."

"All right, Nick. Here's the money for the kids' backpacks. Don't say a word about this to anybody. Don't tell Jen. Don't tell anybody."

"What the hell's going on around here, dude?"

"Nobody knows, Nicky. Nobody knows."

On Wednesday evening at eight o'clock, a nondenominational prayer vigil was held for Renee Sears at St. Mary's Church on Monmouth Street. St. Mary's is the largest church in Gloucester City. Every pew was filled. Local ministers opened the vigil with prayers, then requested testimonials from Renee's friends so the community could "gain an understanding of the precious life force that is hidden from us." A guidance counselor from the high school moderated the testimonials.

Renee's College Biology teacher said that Renee was bound for glory, a girl who outshone the brightest boys in science, technology, engineering, and math.

She predicted Renee would be a disruptive influence in male-dominated Silicon Valley one day. A young man said that Renee's heart was as beautiful as her gorgeous green eyes. The director of the school musical stated that she hoped to put on a production of *The Little Mermaid* in the spring to take advantage of Renee's vocal gifts. Friends spoke of her loyalty, her ability to keep a secret, her inner beauty, her outer beauty, her sweet shyness, her sense of humor, her large vocabulary. Members of the marching band spoke of the void Renee left in the flute line and how her absence from practice each day made the group less of a band and less of a family. The girls' soccer coach said Renee was the first to volunteer to referee local youth soccer games each Sunday. The guidance counselor said he imagined Renee as a doctor one day, or perhaps a zoologist. She was pure. She was innocent. She was strong. She was kind. She was super smart. She was always willing to lend a hand. She was beautiful. She was a candle in the wind, the calm amidst the storm, the straw that stirred the drink, and the wind beneath their wings. A minister led a hopeful prayer and joked that the vigil had only ten minutes left before violating the town curfew. Then the guidance counselor introduced the final student speaker of the evening, Anthony Stanton. More than a few people gritted their teeth and drew a sharp breath when Anthony walked down the side aisle toward the giant statue of St. Joseph and took the microphone.

"Some of you might think I have a lot of guts standing up here speaking about Renee. I wish I could have done something, anything, to save her on Friday. Renee's so innocent that she went chasing after the wolves like they were corgis. Many of you spoke about Renee's sunny side. I'm lucky to know her shadow side: her fears, her insecurities, her doubts about herself, and her doubts about life. I don't speak of Renee in the past tense because I know she's still alive. I can feel her in my heart. I never knew what love was until I met Renee. I never knew what honesty was, what trust was, what being dependable meant—I'd never seen any of those things before until I saw them in her. I wanted to be like her. I've spent my whole life trying to hide my faults from others. I never hid my weaknesses around Renee, and because she didn't run away from them I stopped running away from them. I started facing them and trying to fix them. Want to know why? Because I wanted to be good enough to deserve to be her friend. Thank you for letting me talk."

Chapter Fourteen

Diego Gonzalez was a first-generation law enforcement officer in Mexico. His parents worked as food vendors on the streets of Mexico City, selling stuffed gorditas, tamales, and tacos with carnitas. His parents were on their feet from sunrise to sunset. They took one holiday a year—Christmas. Diego's older brother, Arturo, also worked a food stand, cooking tlacoyos stuffed with braised pork belly, queso fresco cheese, and hot red salsa in Toluca, a town forty miles west of Mexico City. Arturo had five children before he turned thirty. Diego had a beautiful older sister, Lupita, who was his primary caretaker during his entire childhood. His parents worked and worked and worked, and Lupita loved him in their absence. Lupita had a checklist of essential skills she felt every boy should master and worked hard every day teaching them to Diego: his letters, his numbers, how to read, how to dribble a soccer ball, how to add and subtract, and how to hit a pitched ball (the bat was a piece of wood that formerly propped up their clothesline, sawed in half by Lupita). She felt these skills were necessary for Diego to compete on level ground with other boys. By the time he entered high school, Diego was mature and capable. Lupita's instructions were so successful that he no longer needed her attention and care.

Lupita dreaded a future serving street food. She became mesmerized by the money and excitement provided by Luis Martinez, a handsome local thug who delivered large quantities of methamphetamine to south Texas. Lupita completely disappeared from Diego's life when she cast her fate with Luis. She was fearless and intent on escaping the fate of her parents. Their mother often said Lupita had a "harder bark" than her brothers.

Diego had not heard from Lupita in seven years. When Diego joined the police force, he asked police officers throughout Tamaulipas if they had seen her. He presumed she was dead or working as a prostitute in another part of Mexico.

Diego was twenty-seven years old. He began his career as a police officer in Mexico City after passing the Mexican national police vetting exam in 2010. His aptitude and trustworthiness had captured the attention of federal law enforcement officials, and he joined Mexico's Federal Ministerial Police in 2015. Gonzalez thought that the higher perch of a federal police officer would make it easier to locate his sister. It hadn't. He loved his sister and never missed a chance to inquire about her when he made new connections with law enforcement officials throughout Mexico.

Law enforcement positions in Mexico are poorly paid and dangerous. Diego pondered moving to Los Angeles and seeking employment at a private security firm. He welcomed this opportunity to work with the FBI in Philadelphia. Gonzalez was dining alone at the Blue Corn restaurant in Philadelphia's Italian

Market, drinking draft Negra Modelos and eating ceviche de pulpo. He watched a soccer game on a television behind the bar. A middle-aged Mexican woman entered and asked if she could join him at his table. It puzzled him at first. She was considerably older, and there were many empty seats at four that afternoon.

"Can I help you with anything?" he asked.

"I believe that you can. My name is Ana. Like you, I am from Mexico and visiting Philadelphia."

Gonzalez listened but did not respond.

"Your name is Diego, yes?"

"Yes."

"Do you have a sister Lupita?"

Gonzalez was silent.

"I think that we can work together in a way that will be mutually beneficial. As a gesture of good will, I have located your sister in Jalisco. It is, as you know, an unstable, volatile area. She is not in good shape. I don't believe you would recognize her. Take a look," she said, holding up her cell phone. Gonzalez did recognize his sister, but her considerable beauty had been eroded by years of drug abuse and self-neglect.

"Who are you?" he asked.

"I have played the part of a good Samaritan with your sister. It was a delicate situation at first, but I managed to convince her to enter a rehab. First, however, she must endure a rather grueling seven days at a detox facility in Mexico City. If you are willing to help me, Lupita will receive treatment in a private drug rehabilitation facility in Malibu, California. Private psychologists, art therapists, exceptional in every way. The facility demands a minimum twenty-eight-day stay at two thousand dollars a day. If you help me, I will pay for sixty days."

"I assumed she was dead," Gonzalez said, briefly losing his composure.

"She nearly was dead," Ana said. "Now she may have a chance to be reborn. When she becomes healthy enough at the rehab, a sober-living facility will be available in Oregon. They have Twelve Step meetings on site, sobriety coaches, and staff therapists available around the clock. I recommend that your sister not return to the turmoil in Mexico. Perhaps we can work together to relocate her. Who knows, she may decide to become a drug counselor herself."

"Why are you doing this?"

"I have done all of this, Diego, with absolutely no strings attached. Extricating Lupita from Jalisco was messy. I do not think you could have done what I had to do to free her. After she detoxes, she can move on to Malibu if you agree to help me."

"But why? I'm very grateful, but I do not understand how you found me, how you found Lupita, or why you are willing to spend a small fortune to help her."

"You can do something for me, Diego. It will not cost you a penny and comes with further financial incentives. Finish your beer and we'll take a walk."

Gonzalez paid the check and they walked to Bardascino Park at 10th and Carpenter Street. They sat on a bench and Ana stood, lifted her blouse, and pirouetted, exposing a taut stomach and a firm back.

"What are you doing?" Gonzalez asked.

"Just want to make it clear that this is no attempt at entrapment. I am not wearing any kind of recording device. I will give you my cell phone. Disable it until we are finished speaking."

"I'm confused."

"Turn off my phone, please."

"Ok, I did."

"You are working as a law enforcement agent in Mexico for wages that would be insulting to a cab driver in Philadelphia. The narcos are better armed and better equipped, so your profession is dangerous and risky."

"What are you getting at, please?"

"My brother is Esteban Gracias."

"Esteban Gracias. How could I be of any assistance to you? He is locked in a fortress with absolutely no chance of escaping, trust me."

"I only ask you for information. I am committed to spending a quarter of a million dollars to give your sister a chance at a new life. I have rescued Lupita from an early grave, perhaps. I need information. Where this fortress is located? It is not in Canaan, Pennsylvania, as the authorities say."

"He is not in Canaan."

"Will you please repay me by telling me where he is being held?"

"I need to think it over."

"There's no time to think it over, Diego. My brother is being transferred very soon to stand trial in Brooklyn."

"Your brother is in Philadelphia. Held in a secret secure subterranean cell, a concrete bunker designed to hold terrorists. Built beneath a shuttered church. There is an ongoing fight between developers who want to tear down the church building and preservationists who are fighting to preserve it. Neither side realizes they are taking part in a charade. The underground facility is encased in PAXCON and other bomb mitigation and fragmentation materials. It is impenetrable. It has doors similar to those of a nuclear missile silo. It is designed for holding high-value terrorists. It cannot be compromised."

"I realize that. I plan to free my brother while he is en route to Brooklyn. Once he is placed in an American prison, my attempt will be futile. Will you inquire about the logistics of his transfer? Date? Time? Security? I will reward you generously. Let's meet here on Friday at four o'clock."

86

"Okay."

"You can visit your sister in Malibu after September fifteenth."

Chapter Fifteen

Anthony walked into the Gloucester police station and saw a group of strangers: forensics techs, a federal officer from Mexico, County Prosecutor's staff, the mayor, and a host of reporters gathering for the press conference at five o'clock.

"Doesn't even feel like the same place any more. Feels like I'm at a New York City police station," he said to the chief's secretary.

"Hello, Anthony," she said. "I was going to tell you this is a bad time, but every hour is a bad time these days. What can I do for you?"

"Can I talk with Detective O'Brien for a minute?"

"Let me see if he's free."

O'Brien came out of the conference room.

"You must have read my mind, Anthony. I was thinking about stopping by your house. Let's go sit in the in my office for a minute."

"This place is buzzing."

"What's up, buddy?"

"You don't have to tell me the specifics, but did you guys find out any more information about Renee?" Anthony asked.

"I can't talk about it much but, yes, there's been new developments. Small ones but encouraging ones."

"Think she's still alive?"

"Yes, I do. Let me ask you something. Did you notice a black van Friday night, the night you saw the wolves? Maybe a black van in the parking lot at the fields or parked on the street somewhere?" O'Brien asked.

"No, but want to hear something crazy? You know that old drunk who hangs outside the bank asking everyone for money?"

"Chick Austen?"

"Yeah. He told Ottie that he was sleeping in a baseball dugout at the high school and saw the wolves get into the back of a black van."

"Who told you that?"

"Ottie told me yesterday."

"Listen, buddy, anything you hear from now on, no matter how crazy, let me know right away."

"Seemed a little too crazy, wolves getting into a van."

Wednesday's press conference began at five o'clock, with Chief Moran at the podium. Mike Scher had been called away to Washington and was unable to attend. The press was subdued. It was an uneventful day.

"Developments from the past twenty-four hours: A forty-year-old White male,

John Caseban, was found dead in a wooded area behind the Gloucester Swim Club yesterday at approximately seven p.m. A passerby had called 911 after seeing a human body part on Collings Road. Mr. Caseban was the hunter who killed one of the wolves early Tuesday morning. We urge all residents to refrain from hunting these wolves. The forensic scientists at the Camden County Prosecutor's Office have concluded that both Mr. Caseban and Mr. Devlin died from wounds consistent with wolf attacks. The remains of the wolf that Mr. Caseban killed yesterday were taken to the DNA Casework Unit of the FBI. I will brief you on the DNA results when I receive them. Agent Scher is in Washington this evening, so I'll answer any questions that you have."

"Chief Moran, have there been any further sightings of the wolves?"

"None that we've substantiated."

"I know it's farfetched, Chief, but do you think the killing of John Caseban was vengeful?"

"I do not believe that, no."

"Like maybe they hunted the hunter?"

"You're asking if these wolves can engage in higher level complex thinking?"

"Yes."

"I sure the hell hope not," Moran said.

Ana walked into the Betty Mim's Bakery at Broad and Susquehanna Street in Philadelphia. Perfect, she thought, only one person working. She had paid a succession of small bribes to bartenders, barbers, and a young man hanging outside the Safe Streets Center in West Philadelphia to track down Jerome "Bigfoot" Brailey, a street hustler with a long, successful career in the Philadelphia underworld.

"We getting ready to close, ma'am."

Ana put a hundred dollar bill on the bakery counter and asked the young woman if she knew where Jerome Brailey might be.

"He ain't been in here in a while but the bartender at the Cleftone Bar at 27th and South, name's Grady. He'll know. Anybody looking for Jerome can leave a message with Grady at the Cleftone."

Ana drove to the bar and spoke with Grady. She put a hundred dollar bill on the bar and Grady slipped it into his hand.

"What you need Bigfoot for?"

"From what I understand, he's the man to see when someone needs a job done."

"Guess according to what kind of job you speaking about."

"A man at Junior's Barber Shop told me his specialties are robbery, drug distribution, organizing craps games, and then having his confederates rob them."

"He don't do much of that stuff anymore. He mellow now. Still nobody to trifle with."

"Mellow or not, I'd like to see him. I'll give you two hundred dollars if you call him and set up a meeting for tomorrow. Any time, any place. Will you do that, Grady?"

"Let me step in the back for a minute."

He returned with good news.

"Bigfoot said he'll meet you tomorrow at twelve noon at Mr. Silk's Third Base Lounge, up on 52nd Street in West Philly. Bigfoot just bought the place. Said if you expecting him to do a job for you, bring a ten thousand dollar retainer fee."

Ana palmed two hundred dollar bills onto the bar and headed back to Gloucester.

Chapter Sixteen

Jerome "Bigfoot" Brailey was renovating Mr. Silk's Third Base Lounge, a prominent 1960s Philadelphia night club, for a planned Thanksgiving Eve reopening. It was now his headquarters, his first legitimate business after a long succession of lucrative street hustles. He wore a black and white Kith Sport jacket, a green knit shirt, and a pair of Ronnie Fieg–designed Air Maestro II kicks. Ana charged in at noon, ready for some serious negotiations and strategizing.

"What do you think of the ambience?" Jerome asked.

Ana shrugged.

"Was the place to be back in the '60s. Guy named Silky owned the joint. Silky sold lingerie out of his car trunk: 'Stockings to Step-Ins from Mr. Silk.' He parlayed that money, savings from his day job, and a loan from a neighborhood numbers banker to open up this place."

"Fascinating. Can we sit down and talk business? My name is Ana."

"Whole street used to be jammed with late-model Cadillacs and Rolls Royces. Stevie Wonder was here, Teddy Pendergrass, Muhammed Ali. Pimps and hustlers in diamond rings and wide-brimmed hats sitting under the same roof as straight-laced White businessmen and politicians. Silky's was the place to get things done."

"How about you and I start getting things done? I will offer you the most lucrative payday of your life."

"I doubt that, but go ahead. Give me some details."

"A potential million dollar payday."

"You've got my full attention."

"My brother is being held in a secret subterranean security bunker in Philadelphia. He will be transferred to a prison in Brooklyn in a few days to face trial for charges that will result in many consecutive life sentences."

"Is he a terrorist? I ain't freeing a terrorist."

"He is not a terrorist. Stop talking nonsense. Can you put together a team capable of overpowering a federal security detail? I assume you have a crew of some sort, some manpower?"

"Got the best crew in Philadelphia. Got a team of former military special ops guys. But you're talking extremely high risk. Sharpshooters, explosives, gun battles with high-caliber weapons, federal cops, state cops, local cops, prison guards. Asking for a miracle. I've performed a few, but a million dollars seems a little low."

"Make it two million. I will give you until four o'clock Friday to put together a crew and a workable plan," Ana said.

"You gonna tell me where all this is happening?" Jerome asked.

"In Philadelphia. At 1121 Spring Garden Street. It's an abandoned church beneath which federal authorities have built a fortified concrete barracks."

"They did all that just for your brother?"

"They did it anticipating potentially holding terrorists. They are holding my brother there because he has broken out of prison a number of times."

"What line of work is he in?"

"Can you handle this job?"

"I have marksmen and men experienced with a wide range of explosives. Got access to war-grade weapons. Credit cards that have been approved and verified by big banks under fake names, phony driver's licenses, library cards, everything needed to substantiate a false identity. We can rent a couple of trucks and dump them when the job's done and they can't be traced back to us."

"I'm desperate because of the short time frame. I thought I had months to put this together. I have days."

"Do you also have a crew of your own, or is this exclusively a Jerome Brailey production?"

"I have a two-man crew. They will be as effective as anyone you have."

"What's their specialty?"

"Killing people."

"Will I get to meet them? How am I going to integrate them into the plan?"

"We can talk about it tomorrow," Ana said.

"What's the terms of the deal? When's payday?"

Ana removed an envelope from her purse.

"Here is a ten thousand dollar retainer. The remainder depends on how feasible your plan is."

"My plan will be feasible, workable, and effective. I'm the only guy in Philly who can pull this off. But if I do it, I'm going to have to get out of town for a long while. I have a couple of profitable enterprises that I'll be forced to abandon. Gonna be a cost factored in for that, too. Price tag's three million dollars. Cash. And I ain't brushing my teeth Saturday until it's in my possession."

"Anything else?"

"I don't work or play well with others. You know what my favorite time of day is? When nobody knows where I'm at or what I'm doing. So if this is my operation, it's *my* operation. Too many cooks spoil the broth."

"Fair enough. See you tomorrow at four."

The moment Ana was out the door, Jerome was on the phone to his partner, Yvonne, parked a hundred feet down the block.

"You see her?"

"She's getting into black van with two Mexican men."

"Follow her and see where else she goes. Anywhere she stops, copy down the address. Don't let her see you. But if she pulls any kind of evasive maneuver, keep driving. She's high-strung."

"What's your impression?"

"Oh, she's formidable. Gotta be careful. Good thing is, she's pressed for time, too nervous to think straight. Would not want to go head-to-head with her when she wasn't nervous. Get an address and call me."

Chapter Seventeen

Hanging at Ottie's had lost its tang, Anthony felt. Just wasn't the same without Renee. He shot some hoops at the basketball courts at Johnson and Hudson, then walked to Heritage's and bought an Orange Fanta and a soft pretzel. Coming out the door, he spotted a black van pull up to the curb across Broadway from Heritage's. He picked up his pace. The van dropped off two men at a boarding house on Broadway and headed north. He threw the food into a trashcan and jogged on the sidewalk down Broadway.

The van passed Middlesex Street and stopped at a red light at Mercer, obscured momentarily by a late-model Lexus driven by a woman wearing an Adidas baseball cap. Anthony quickened his pace. The van reappeared and turned left onto Mercer toward the river. Gloucester has a series of alternating one-way streets, so Anthony climbed the laundromat steps and peered down Mercer, waiting to see if the van turned left or right. The van turned left onto King Street and Anthony sprinted down Broadway to Middlesex to see if the van continued south along King Street or turned up Middlesex toward Broadway. The van turned left on Middlesex. He saw headlights approaching. Anthony crouched behind a car, staring at the van as it parked in front of a two-story brick row house.

A white-haired Mexican woman exited the van, unlocked the front door of a house, and went inside. Anthony waited five minutes and walked up Middlesex toward King Street. An identical row of brick houses stood on the other side of the 200 block of Middlesex. Anthony turned at Willow Street and ran through unfenced backyards to gain a vantage point across the street from the black van. A house with crumbling brick face had particle board nailed across the back door and windows. It looked abandoned.

Anthony pushed at the basement windows with his foot. One window was unlocked. He dropped to the ground and went in feet first. He landed in a dank basement and ran up the cellar steps, imagining rats scurrying after him in the dark. The floorboards on the first floor were rotted. He stepped carefully across the floor and tiptoed up the stairway to the second floor and peered out a curtainless window. This vantage point provided a clear view of the house across the street. A light was on in the back of the house, but he couldn't detect any movement inside. He stood staring for ten minutes, debating whether to call Detective O'Brien. He heard a noise in the basement. Someone was climbing the cellar steps. He heard the rotted floorboards squeaking in the living room. The someone was climbing the steps to the second floor.

"Holy snap," he thought. "Why didn't I call O'Brien?" He got down on his knees and crouched in a corner, breathing through his mouth and praying. The weight on the steps told him an adult was approaching. He heard a woman singing

"Never Can Say Goodbye" by the Jackson 5. Anthony peeked through the opening of the door. It was the lady with the Adidas baseball cap from the Lexus. She walked into the room and stared out the window, turned and saw him kneeling on the floor.

"Hell's the matter with you? You homeless?"

"Nah, I…," he began.

"Really sorry to be bursting in on y'all. You alone?"

"Yeah."

"Hiding from the law?"

"Nah, it's a long story," Anthony said. Standing but keeping his distance.

"What street is this?" she asked.

"Middlesex Street."

"So that house over there is 212 Middlesex Street? Middlesex with an 'M?'"

"Yes."

"My name's Yvonne," she said, extending a manicured right hand.

"Anthony."

"Anthony, I've got to make a phone call."

She spoke on the phone, "Yo, I followed her across the bridge. She's in a little town. Anthony, what's the name of this town?"

"Gloucester."

"She's at 212 Middlesex Street in Gloucester. That's my new friend, Anthony. Jerome says 'hello.' We're in an abandoned house across the street from the lady. She dropped off the two bodyguards a couple of blocks away. I can't see nothing in the dark. She's got a light on in the back but the angle's not good enough to see inside. What do you want me to do?"

She paused, then continued, "Anthony, Jerome wants to know if you want a job? Pay you twenty dollars an hour to do the overnight shift spying on the lady who went into the house."

"Definitely."

"Anthony is joining the team. Talk to you when I get back," Yvonne said, ending the call. "Anthony, you like the Jacksons?"

"Michael Jackson and them? Yeah. As much as I know them. I like Kendrick Lamar and Meek Mill."

"I'm gonna give you some homework tonight. School start yet?"

"Next week."

"You got earbuds for your phone?"

"Yeah."

"When you're standing here spying, listen to some Jackson 5. Keep you awake. Why you spying on the house, anyway?"

"They kidnapped my friend."

"Who kidnapped your friend? That Mexican bitch?"

"You hear about the wolf attacks in Gloucester?"

"That's where we're at? Where the wolves are loose? Shit. Figures."

"We were the first people to see them, my friend and me. Last Friday. My friend wanted to pet them and that's the last time we saw her."

"Pet a wolf? White people do some crazy shit."

"Think I should call the cops?"

"Do NOT call the cops. N-O! Lemme call Jerome. He'll know what to do."

She called Jerome again. He knew the story of the wolf attacks and asked if Anthony could ride over to Silky's with Yvonne.

"Tell him he's on the clock. Twenty dollars an hour. No sense him telling you, you telling me, me relaying my answers to you, you relaying the answers to him. Just bring him over and we can talk," Jerome said.

"You able to take a ride to Philly with me?" Yvonne asked.

"Yeah."

"Jerome says you're on the clock. Gonna be a good payday for you."

"I'm up for that."

They climbed out the basement window and got into Yvonne's car.

"Let's listen to some Jackson 5. How about 'Maybe Tomorrow?' I got a cassette player installed in this baby because I do NOT like digital music. I'm an analog-only girl. What grade you going in?"

"Tenth?"

"What's your mom and dad do?"

"My dad ain't been around in years. I never see him."

"Join the club. Ain't seen mine in so long, couldn't even tell you what he looks like. How about your mom?"

"She's a bartender in Cherry Hill. She's cool. Gets me what I want. She's got her own issues."

"Don't we all. You're smart to realize."

They drove across the bridge to the Third Base Lounge.

"Hey, hey, hey. What have we here?" Jerome greeted them. "You must be Anthony."

Anthony nodded and shook his hand.

"Let's sit down and talk, Anthony. Welcome to Mr. Silk's Third Base Lounge, reopening on Thanksgiving Eve. Excuse the mess. This place had a previous incarnation in the 1960s. Everybody who was anybody hung here. Muhammed Ali, Stevie Wonder, Teddy Pendergrass."

"Anthony doesn't even know who any of those guys are, Bigfoot." Yvonne said.

"I know Muhammed Ali."

"See? He knows," Jerome said.

"Why do they call you 'Bigfoot?' Your feet look normal," Anthony said.

"Well, Anthony, I inherited somebody else's nickname because I had the same given name as him. My name is Jerome Brailey. Another Jerome Brailey, Jerome 'Bigfoot' Brailey, occupied the drum seat for Parliament Funkadelic, the Chambers Brothers, the Unifics, the Five Stairsteps, all great '60s soul and funk bands. If you ever see episode nine of *Soul Train*, November 27, 1971, you can see my namesake in action. They called him 'Bigfoot,' and somewhere along the line, they started calling me 'Bigfoot.' You can call me Jerome. Yvonne only calls me 'Bigfoot' when she's annoyed at me. It's like a tell in a poker game. Tips me off that she's mad."

"I ain't mad. You just talk too much. Think the kid wants to hear all this shit?"

"All right, let's get down to the real nitty gritty. Tell me about these wolves."

"They killed a hunter in Gloucester, plus another guy taking a leak behind a bar. My friend Renee went to pet them, and we haven't seen her since. It'll be a week tomorrow. I saw the wolves myself with Renee, but I was afraid of them and went the other way."

"Smart kid."

"Some old drunk in Gloucester told my friend he saw the wolves get into the back of that lady's van."

104

"Man, that is unsettling. Craziest thing I ever heard," Jerome said. "Wolves riding around in a van."

"You better bring the wolves up next time you talk with her," Yvonne said.

"I intend to. I'm meeting with her tomorrow at four."

"Anthony thinks his friend is being held by the woman," Yvonne said.

"You a member of our team now, Anthony. Full-fledged. Don't see what they'd need with a little girl. How old is she?" Jerome asked.

"Fifteen."

"Here's what I think," Yvonne said. "Lady might be holding Renee to use as a shield during the jailbreak, figuring cops ain't likely to shoot a young White girl whose face has been all over the news."

"Or she figures nobody's going to shoot at the vehicle knowing this little girl's with them," Jerome said.

"Lady's been seeing the big picture since the day she arrived, thinking five steps ahead of everybody," Yvonne said.

"She's a bad bitch," Jerome said. "Felt that the minute I met her. Nobody to trifle with."

"Gonna have to be on our game," Yvonne said.

"Anthony, think you can go back up in that abandoned house and keep an eye on things? Any movement by the lady, call Yvonne. I'm gonna need Yvonne over here. We only have two days to plan our operation."

"Yeah, sure. Maybe I'll spot Renee."

"Here's four hundred dollars for your trouble and my cell number. And Yvonne's cell number. You play baseball, Anthony?"

"I played Little League."

"Guess what our motto is at Mr. Silk's Third Base Lounge? 'Gotta touch Third Base before you go home.' What do you think?"

"I like it."

"Tell Yvonne that on your way back to Gloucester. She thinks it's corny."

"I think you're corny," Yvonne said. "Let's go, Anthony. Getting late, honey."

Chapter Eighteen

Yvonne dropped Anthony off on Mercer Street. He walked to the house with the crumbling brick face and crawled through the basement window, jogged across the gloomy basement, and resumed his watch from the second floor. Right before midnight, Ana exited the house, locked the door, and drove toward Broadway. Anthony called Yvonne.

"She just left."

"Probably time to walk the wolves. Call me when she gets back."

Ana picked up the diableros at the boarding house and drove to Philadelphia.

"Time to create a major diversion for the Philadelphia Police Department. Some entertainers are filming a YouTube video in Philadelphia. Obnoxious rich kids embarrassing people walking down the street. *The Savage Skins Show*, they call it. Let's inject some real savagery. Create a massive problem for the Philadelphia police to spend their energies resolving. The more havoc, the better. Give them something that will take days to clean up and require lots of manpower," Ana said.

She dropped the diableros off in an alley behind a movie theater at 2nd and Walnut Street in the Society Hill section of Philadelphia. The diableros walked to the film shoot in human guise. It was one in the morning. The street was cordoned off by police and lit by medium-arc iodide lamps to simulate daytime. A large group of teenage girls held iPhones in their outstretched arms, making personal videos. Camera operators were visible and a group of perfectly coiffed, baby-faced twenty-somethings were giggling in anticipation of an upcoming prank. Other actors were in the backyard of a Society Hill townhouse, obscured by a six-foot wooden fence erected for the scene. As the diableros walked past, one of the actors catapulted off a trampoline in the yard, flew over the fence and landed on the diableros, knocking them to the ground. The diableros were stunned. When they attempted to get back on their feet, the boy-group wannabes blew fire balls at them from a mix of butane, dish soap, and cornstarch in their palms.

"You're being attacked by dragons," they shouted as the show's camera operators recorded the humiliation. "We're the Savage Skins. You came at us at your own risk."

The diableros were disoriented and stumbled past the teenage girls, who were laughing hysterically, still recording on their iPhones. The men circled the block, transformed, and charged back to the scene. Both wolves attacked the actor who landed on them, tearing off his face and his limbs. They attacked the boy-band wannabes, dissembling their bodies, spraying blood and viscera. They attacked the camera crew, one of whom filmed their approach, dropping the camera when his throat was torn apart. The teenage girls continued, even now, to extend their arms and capture the violence on their phones. They thought it was just another prank from the Savage Skins. When the wolves turned their yellow eyes and bloody muzzles in their direction, the teens realized too late that some games couldn't be rigged. The wolves tore through their cropped pants and Steve Madden booties. The carnage lasted until the street corner was empty. Police found sixteen bodies scattered along the cobblestone street. Forensics techs spent twelve hours matching body parts and identifying the deceased, a daunting task because most of the faces had been torn off. A passerby lifted a cell phone from the sidewalk and, after discovering the video, posted it on YouTube. It had fifteen million views before noon. The story led all network newscasts Friday morning and was the banner headline on every news site on the internet.

At first word of the news, the Philadelphia media decamped from Gloucester City and assembled in Head House Square, along the outskirts of Society Hill. Philadelphia Police closed the crime scene off from vehicular and pedestrian traffic. FBI agent Mike Scher was assigned to assist the Philadelphia PD with the investigation. He received a call from Chief Moran.

Moran said, "A Mexican woman in a black van is a partner to all of this. She may even be directing it. She's approximately fifty years old. Slender. Thick white hair. The diableros probably traveled to Philly in her van. Have someone review video footage from the toll booths of the Ben Franklin and Walt Whitman bridges. Maybe you'll get a tag number. She's the key."

"Can't believe I have to explain this mumbo jumbo all over again. Should've seen the looks on some of the Philly cops when I started telling them what we're dealing with."

"Better you than me, buddy. Good luck," Moran said, relieved that the situation was not his problem.

Chapter Nineteen

Anthony's phone rang, startling him.

"Hello?"

"Anthony, it's Yvonne. Any sign of that Mexican woman?"

"Shit, I must have fallen asleep. Sorry. Let me look. I don't see the van. Did you see all the stuff that happened in Philly last night? I was watching the video on my phone," Anthony said.

"I saw it. Complete insanity. And Bigfoot's in business with her," Yvonne said.

"Next time she leaves, I'm going to see if I can get into the house. I want to search for my friend."

"Are you crazy? How you gonna do that?" Yvonne asked.

"Bust through a basement window or something."

"Ain't that breaking and entering?"

"I guess. I know the cops, so…"

"So they let you break into houses?"

"No, but I want to see if Renee is at the house," Anthony said.

"Stay the hell away. Who knows what kind of voodoo they got going on. Wanna get torn apart by wolves?"

"I need to go home and take a shower and a nap."

"You just had a nap. Take a quick shower and call me when you get back," Yvonne said.

Anthony started toward home, then turned around, and went into the backyard of 212 Middlesex. His gut told him Renee was in that house. The front door was visible from the street, so he walked around to the back of the house hoping no one would see him. He twisted the back door knob. It was locked. He walked along the perimeter of the house, pushing the basement windows with his foot. No luck. He decided to break one of the basement windows. He found a chunk of brick and tossed it through a window pane, waited to see if it drew the attention of any neighbors, then reached down to turn the lock handle. He pushed the window open and shimmied into the basement. His heart was pounding. Some bile came up in his throat.

His eyes adjusted to the dark of the basement and he walked around searching for any indication Renee had been there. He picked up a rag on the floor, thinking it might be a piece of her clothing. Just then he heard the front door knob squeak. Someone was attempting to get in. The front door wouldn't open. Anthony sensed movement around the outside of the house, then heard the back door knob turn. Two male voices expressed frustration. Anthony crouched beneath the cellar steps. Whoever was outside spotted the open window and began their own descent into the basement. A pair of dirty Nikes appeared through the open window. Anthony panicked. They would detect his scent right away, he feared. He reached into his pocket, pulled out his cell phone, and called O'Brien.

"Detective O'Brien, it's Anthony. I need help. I'm in the basement of 212 Middlesex Street. I found where the Mexican lady lives and broke in looking for Renee and now the wolves are here. Hurry. Please."

"We're coming," O'Brien said.

One of the men had crawled through the window and was in the basement. Anthony closed his eyes and prayed, gaining some time when the second man struggled to get through the narrow window. It sounded like the men were sawing something. He heard metal grating against metal. Then he heard police sirens screaming down Middlesex Street from both directions. Anthony ran up the basement steps, unlocked the back door, and ran into the yard.

"They're in the basement."

Five cops, weapons drawn and in tactical shooting stances, entered the house.

"Put your hands on the wall. Now."

The cops charged the men. Anthony listened at the door, surprised at how docile the men were while being handcuffed. O'Brien came out the back door.

"It's two junkies stealing copper pipe. You know how lucky you are? You would have been torn to shreds before we got here. What the hell were you thinking?"

"I saw the black van parked here. I hung around until the lady left and then I broke in to see if they had Renee."

"Why didn't you call me?" O'Brien demanded.

"I should have called you. I'm sorry. I'm impulsive."

"Get your shit together, dude. We might have shot those junkies."

The cops were putting two hapless drug addicts into the back of the cop cars. The cops glared at him when Anthony made eye contact.

"Anthony, you positive the lady lives here? You broke into somebody's house. Don't ever do that again. Period. No matter what," O'Brien said.

"I'm sorry, really sorry. The lady does live here. Or some Mexican lady with a black van does, anyway."

"That doesn't mean you break into her house. We can't break into her house. We'd have to get a warrant."

"I messed up, big time. I'm sorry."

"All right. Get outta here."

O'Brien went into the basement, locked the window, and secured the back door lock. Anthony walked home. Renee pounded futilely on the double pane attic window as she watched the police cars pull away.

Chapter Twenty

Diego Gonzalez arrived at Bardascino Park in South Philadelphia at four o'clock and saw Ana admiring a mural painted on the side wall.

"I like the street art in this city. Murals everywhere. Reminds me of Mexico City," Ana said.

"It's vibrant. Maybe I'll stay here," Gonzalez said.

"Would be smart. Too dangerous in Mexico to be with the police. Not an acceptable risk for the salary," Ana said.

"I found out information about your brother's transfer. Takes place tomorrow morning. Two identical five-car armored caravans will leave Philadelphia and Canaan at six. The caravan in Canaan is a ruse, of course. The deception is being coordinated by the Justice Prisoner and Alien Transportation System, an agency of the federal government," Gonzalez reported.

"Five armored cars?"

"Five armored cars."

"Will you be part of the detail?

"I will."

"Any way to reveal which vehicle my brother is traveling in tomorrow?"

"I will drop a handkerchief alongside the vehicle your brother is in. I hope to travel in the same vehicle but that may not be possible. It won't be my decision."

"Then you better drop another handkerchief besides the vehicle you're riding in. The rest are getting blown up."

"The streets will be cordoned off with tight security. How will you see the handkerchiefs?"

"I've hired someone to figure that out. Guy named Jerome who smuggled from Turkey through Marseilles for a long time. Involved in a steady stream of criminal activity in Philadelphia for decades. He was recommended to me by someone I trust. Told me Jerome can do the job, if anyone can," Ana explained.

"High-risk, low-probability operations require intelligence and daring. Seems like a smart choice. Know his plan for tomorrow?" Gonzalez asked.

"I'm meeting with him later this afternoon. Please, I must know if there are any changes on the logistics of the transfer. This first plan may be a charade. Here's a clean cell phone with only one number programmed, mine. Put it into a public trash receptacle first chance you get after we free my brother. I put a canvas bag under the bench in front of the mural. For your troubles," Ana said, nodding toward the other side of the small park. "Contact me if something significant changes."

Chapter Twenty-One

Ana glided through the doors of the Third Base Lounge. Jerome sat alone, listening to Sly and The Family Stone through the tavern's sound system.

"Ana, do you know sound waves travel in different dimensions? Every time someone kisses someone while listening to a song, the guy or girl who wrote the song gets a shiver through their spine. A hot and cold feeling both at once. I imagine Sly got that feeling a lot, back in the day."

"Can we talk business instead of lunacy?"

"I'm all business from here on out."

"Do you have enough manpower to handle five armored cars? They will transfer my brother at six a.m. tomorrow."

"Well, I spent the advance you gave me wisely. Spent it a few times. Excuse me a minute while I retrieve something I picked up for the operation—a rocket-propelled grenade launcher for the birthday party tomorrow. Got four of them."

"And you have people who know how to use them?" Ana asked.

"Got guys who spent six months as mercenaries in Syria. RPGs are like slingshots over there. Everybody and their cousin got one."

"Who else is working? Operational details, please."

"I'll have someone on the roof of a church, 'bout ten blocks away, looking through Swarovski Rangefinding binoculars. Ever try a pair? Swarovskis are so powerful, we could watch them drive all the way to Brooklyn if we weren't going to blow them up first. Three grand for a pair of binoculars. Can see fifteen hundred yards like it's a yard away. Rain proof. Fog proof."

"Sounds impressive."

"I have sharpshooters and machine gunners, veterans of heavy action in the Middle East. This is gonna be just another day at the office for 'em. I got weapons that will disable the armored vehicles. Now, how am I going to know which vehicle be carrying your brother?"

"A man will drop a handkerchief next to the car that holds my brother."

"Gonna take out the other four vehicles with those RPGs," Jerome said.

Ana looked at her phone and said, "Before we proceed further, I want to warn you that if anything goes wrong tomorrow, you will be hunted, tortured, and killed. Mind if I film you for a moment?"

"Be my guest."

Ana filmed Jerome and sent the video back to her people in Mexico. Then she FaceTimed her brother's bodyguards in Mexico, showing Jerome a group of fifteen men in a pool hall, glaring at the screen menacingly. Ana said, "If anything happens to my brother or me, these men will hunt you without cease, and when they find you, you will wish you'd never been born."

"I wished that a number of times already. Spin that camera around again and I'll invite them to Silky's. 'Gotta touch Third Base before you go home.'"

"I'd appreciate a bit more gravity, Mr. Brailey. Life-and-death season has arrived. I'm paying you a fortune to free my brother."

"Money well spent. If they leaving at six, let's meet at an empty parking lot behind a roller derby hall at 9th and Callowhill. Be there at four a.m. I'll have somebody cut the gate chains and let us all in. We can rendezvous there. Close enough to get right over to the church if they decide to leave early. Every business is out of business in that neighborhood. No police patrols ever."

"Agreed. Four a.m. 9th and Callowhill."

"You are responsible for moving your brother once everyone else is eliminated, correct?"

"Correct."

"You are responsible for providing your own getaway vehicle, correct?"

"Correct."

"Gonna be a massive manhunt. Don't waste time with goodbyes."

"You will never see me again," Ana said.

"How about those two bodyguards of yours? They working tomorrow?"

"They will be working for me. They can cause quite a bit of havoc very rapidly, so everything better go exactly as you detail. They caused the commotion at the television shoot earlier this morning. I'm sure you've seen it on social media or the news. They will eliminate anyone who exits a vehicle at 9th and Callowhill, so no surprises please."

"I call all the shots until your brother is free, correct?"

"Correct."

"The operation's gonna take a hundred and twenty seconds," Jerome said.

"Meet you at 9th and Callowhill," Ana replied.

"Hold up. When's payday? Told you I ain't getting out of bed 'til I'm holding the money. Don't want a wire transfer because the government will freeze it. I want cash."

"Soon as we arrive tomorrow at four, I provide three million dollars cash. Remain in your vehicle. Someone will bring it to you."

"Long as it ain't one of those wolves. See you tomorrow morning."

Jerome called Yvonne.

"She's leaving. Don't follow her. Call Anthony and make sure he's watching her house. Tell him to call you when she gets there. I want to know if the bodyguards are with her. And tell Anthony we need him over here tonight. Pick him up at seven at his real house. She pull away yet?"

"You talk so much, she's probably halfway across the damn bridge."

"Call Anthony."

Soon after, Yvonne walked into Silky's, grabbed a bottle of beer from the ice chest, and sat down.

"What'd the lady say?" Yvonne asked.

"We meet at 9th and Callowhill at four tomorrow morning. Says she's giving me the money tomorrow. I was born at night, but it wasn't last night. What she's planning is that after we free her brother, the wolves tear our asses apart. She grabs her money back and returns to Mexico."

"Underestimating the intelligence of a Black man. Ain't the first."

"Ain't gonna be the last neither. Talk to Anthony? He good working tomorrow?"

"He good. Gonna miss that little man."

"Been a good soldier."

When Yvonne arrived with Anthony two hours later, Jerome said, "You wanna be there for the fireworks tomorrow? Thinking the lady might bring your friend along."

"Definitely, yes. You think she has Renee?"

"That's my gut instinct. Might be using her tomorrow as a human shield or something. Thought you might want to be around to help rescue her."

"Definitely."

"Got it all worked out. Safety first. No one is leaving her vehicle except the girl. Got a couple of guys, ex-Marine snipers in Iraq, gonna be set up on the roof of a big-ass factory on the next block. Night vision scopes pointed right at the vehicle. Anybody gets outta that van but your friend, they gonna have an extra hole in they head, compliments of me."

"Can't wait to see Renee."

"And I can't wait to see my money. Gonna give you a nice cut, too. After the operation tomorrow morning, we come back here, make sure everybody's okay, go our separate ways. Yvonne and I gonna have to split this scene for a while. Might be some angry narcos looking for us. Hey, Yvonne!"

"Bigfoot!"

"Let's go over the logistics one more time."

"I'm listening."

"We got Donnell and Bunchie up on the factory roof with sniper rifles. Got Ronnie waiting with that rocket-propelled grenade launcher. Got Lee and Snapper behind the little luncheonette across 9th Street with modified AK-47s. She drive that rickety black van, won't even have to open the doors. Be like shooting through a can of tuna."

"Make sure Anthony's friend is in our car before anybody fires a shot," Yvonne said.

"Hope she ain't already in heaven," Jerome said.

"I got a bad feeling, Big. Ana seems too smart to walk into a trap like this. Better be careful," Yvonne said.

"Oh, she plenty smart, but she desperate. Playing a bad hand. Those armored cars carrying her brother? Gonna be bomb proof, bullet proof, every other proof. Impossible dream to free him. Glad to take her money though."

"Glad to get Anthony's friend back, too," Yvonne said.

"Whole thing's gonna be over in a minute. I already paid Donnell, Bunchie, and them. Figure things might get a bit crazy. Might have to scatter in different directions right away."

"Counting your chickens before they hatch. Not like you, Big," Yvonne said.

"Seem too easy?"

"Got something up her sleeve, count on it," Yvonne said.

Chapter Twenty-Two

Jerome drove an Audi A6 with enhanced privacy windows through the streets of West Philadelphia.

"Only time the man is ever quiet, Anthony," Yvonne said. "On the way to a job."

"Failing to plan is planning to fail," said Jerome. "And I ain't planning to fail."

They approached the fenced-in parking lot at 9th and Callowhill at three thirty. It was empty. Jerome cut the chains to the parking lot gate and communicated with the snipers and gunners through a head mic.

"Should be here any minute. You see a young white girl, maybe fifteen-years-old. Hold your fire and I'll walk you through what we do next," Jerome said. "Affirm that for me," he paused.

"No shooting if the girl's in the frame."

After a long, silent fifteen minutes, Ana pulled into the lot in a 2016 Mercedes Benz Sprinter 3500 cargo van with heavily tinted windows.

"Lookie here. Ditched that old tin can," Jerome said. "Let's see what her next move is."

Renee stumbled out of the Mercedes, empty-handed and wearing a vest stuffed with C-4 plastic explosives.

"Hold your fire," Jerome said. "Anthony, push that door open for your friend."

Renee entered the Audi.

"Renee!" Anthony said.

"I'm wearing an explosive vest," Renee said. "Ana has her thumb pushed down on the remote control. If she lifts her thumb, we blow up. If someone shoots her, her thumb lifts and we blow up."

"Told you that bitch was gonna try to outwit us," Yvonne said.

"Smell that odor. That's C-4. Shit smells like a skunk," Jerome said.

"You okay, honey?" Yvonne asked Renee.

"No. She's a bad person."

"She gonna be a dead person in five minutes," Jerome said. "How the hell she know how to rig a suicide vest? I should call her bluff."

"You got two fifteen-year-olds ain't even started their lives yet, Bigfoot. Slow down," Yvonne said.

"She had some man hook the vest up this morning," Renee said.

"What'd he look like?" Jerome asked.

"Looked like he'd done it before," Renee said.

"That doesn't sound good," Jerome said.

Anthony and Yvonne comforted Renee.

"Renee, how is that vest attached to your body?" Jerome asked.

"It's got straps in the back," Renee said.

"Anthony, hop up here and sit on Yvonne's lap for a moment. I'm going to squeeze back there with Renee," Jerome said.

"What you doing, Big?" Yvonne asked.

"Gonna cut this vest off Renee. That bitch can't see through these windows. Carry my trusty Kubotan hunting knife for just these occasions. Then I'm gonna walk over and get my money," Jerome answered. He cut through the straps and gingerly lifted the vest from Renee.

"Sure you wanna do this, Big?"

"Long as she ain't got a sniper up there, we good. All right, fellas. It's showtime. Lee and Snap, approach her vehicle now. Lee, take the right side. Snap, take the left. You guys have one job—shooting the wolves. Full focus, full alert. Blast the shit out of those wolves. Donnell, Bunchie, soon as I throw this vest on the roof of the Mercedes, shoot out her tires. We good?"

"We good, Big," Donnell said.

Jerome strutted across the parking lot holding the vest in his left hand and a Sig Sauer P226 in his right. He tossed the vest onto the roof of the Mercedes and walked away. The snipers put a bullet through each of her tires, and Jerome returned to his Audi.

"Her move. Give her five minutes and I'll call in the cavalry. Ronnie, you ready

126

with that grenade launcher?"

The door of the Mercedes burst opened and the wolves charged. One wolf was felled immediately by the snipers and the other wolf was blasted with automatic weapon fire before he could reach either of Jerome's gunmen. Jerome exited his vehicle and walked toward the Mercedes.

"Steer clear of the line of fire, everybody. She in a bad mood."

He walked with his right arm extended, pointing the Sig Sauer at the Mercedes and circling twenty feet in a circumference around the vehicle until he had an angle on Ana. The vest exploded on the roof, sending shards of pebbled windshield and pieces of metal in every direction and knocking Jerome, Lee, and Snapper to the ground.

After twenty seconds, Jerome arose and dusted himself off.

"Spiteful woman just ruined a perfectly good vehicle. Everybody good?"

Jerome reached into the back of the Mercedes and grabbed a large duffle bag.

"Another good day, my friends. Thank you kindly. I'm gonna have to lay low with Yvonne for a while. She ain't even telling me where we're going. Let you know when I'm back in Philly."

The gunmen got into their vehicles and left.

Jerome drove to the Third Base Lounge with Yvonne, Anthony, and Renee. Once inside, Jerome counted out twenty thousand dollars for Anthony. Renee went to the rest room to wash up.

"Gonna give Renee twenty thousand, too," Jerome said.

"Give her twenty thousand of my money, also." Yvonne said. "After what she

been through? Shit."

Jerome was counting out the money for Renee when Diego Gonzalez burst

through the door, gun drawn, Federal Ministerial Police badge in hand.

"Who the hell are you?" Jerome asked.

"I'm Plan C. This means Plan A and Plan B didn't work. I'm here to take back

that money to the men who provided it. You didn't live up to your end of the deal."

"How does a cop from Mexico got jurisdiction over anything happening in

Philadelphia?"

"'Cause I got this in my hand," he said, waving his gun.

"You're the cop I saw in the police chief's office in Gloucester," Anthony said.

"And that makes you expendable," Gonzalez said, aiming his gun at Anthony,

applying pressure on the trigger. "Sorry, kid."

A wolf leaped at Gonzalez, snarling, tearing his neck apart. His gun discharged

into the wall as he fell. The wolf ran into the streets of West Philadelphia and

disappeared.

"Can you make sure Renee is all right in the bathroom, Yvonne?" Anthony

asked.

"She ain't in the bathroom, honey. Might find her clothes in there. They did some of their voodoo to your friend."

"No!" Anthony said.

"Least she's on our side. Just saved your life, for starters," Yvonne said.

"Yvonne, see if this guy's got a cell phone," Jerome said.

Yvonne found one in Gonzalez's side pocket.

"He's got two of them," Yvonne said, digging through his pockets. "One looks like one of those single-use beaters. One's got a ton of contacts on it."

"Dial 911 on his real phone and report that craziness over at 9th and Callowhill. Let the cops think this guy had something to do with it. I'll call Lee and Snapper to clean this mess up. Better get out of here before plan D shows up."

Chapter Twenty-Three

Anthony slept most of Sunday. The disconnect between the events of the past two weeks and his return to high school in two days seemed as wide as a continent. People were celebrating all over social media that Renee had been reunited with her family. It was a joyous moment in Gloucester. Anthony longed to see her but hesitated to contact her. He realized the enormous adjustment she was facing. Reuniting with her family was going to be her primary focus, he told himself. In the past eleven days, Anthony had been interrogated as a suspect in Renee's disappearance, been dumped by his girlfriend, spoken in front of a packed church, broken into a house, helped a Philadelphia gangster, sat at a table with a rocket-propelled grenade launcher laying on top, been briefly reunited with Renee while she was strapped to an explosive vest, watched a shootout, seen two wolves blasted by machine guns, earned twenty thousand dollars, been nearly executed by a corrupt Mexican cop, and witnessed his best friend's metamorphosis into a wolf. He was about to begin his sophomore year of high school.

Like millions of other previously indifferent adolescents, Anthony resolved to become more serious about school this year. On Tuesday, he survived three morning classes and headed to the cafeteria for fourth period lunch. He filled his tray, punched his Free and Reduced Lunch code into the computer, and scanned the cafeteria for suitable company. Gloucester High mixed all grade levels at lunch, so students were not guaranteed to find classmates in their lunch period. Anthony searched for his friends Austin, Shawn, and Tyler and was disappointed to see that his usual lunch crew would not be reconvening this year. He sat by himself at the windows looking onto the varsity football field and then sensed the presence of Renee Sears sitting down across from him.

"Yo, dude," he said.

Renee sat down with her tray. After a short pause, she said, "So, Anthony, how was your summer?"

"Pretty uneventful. How was yours?"

"Do you want to get out of here? Take a walk to the river?"

"Never have to ask me twice, you know that. But it seems a little strange for you to want to ditch school."

"I'm on a half-day schedule until next week. Anticipated rough adjustment and all that."

"So you can just sign out? Sweet. I have to sneak out. Luckily, I've done this a few times in the past. Give me five minutes and I'll meet you behind Wawa."

They avoided main roads and zigzagged down to Proprietor's Park, which nestled the Delaware River. They talked about their schedules, friends, teachers, Anthony's new sneakers, Renee's new haircut, anything but the events of the previous eleven days. They arrived at the park and sat on benches along the outskirts of Freedom Pier, sitting in silence for a moment as they watched a black Labrador going shoulder down on a dead fish and his owner screaming in disgust.

"Can I hug you?" Anthony asked.

"Are you doubting this is me?"

"Can't believe we're sitting here together and you're all right."

"I'm not sure about the 'all right' part. But I'm happy to be here. You won't believe what I've been through."

"Only tell me what you're comfortable talking about."

"I can tell everything to you. But you have to promise it stays between us."

"Haven't said one word to anybody and never will."

"Do you know that the day you broke into the house on Middlesex Street I was locked in the attic?"

"No way, dude."

"I saw you walking away down Willow Street. I was pounding on the windows. Ana had them nailed shut."

"Holy snap. I had a feeling you were in there. I went in to see if you were, but these two crackheads broke in to steal copper pipe and I panicked. I thought it was those Mexican dudes, so I called the cops. No matter what happened to you, I got your back forever. I won't flinch."

"Well, I was locked in a stifling hot attic the whole time. She didn't feed me for the first two days. She threw bottles of water up the steps and then locked the door right away. By the time she put food on the attic steps, I would have eaten tree bark. She left me this stew. I thought it was chili, but it had psychotropic properties."

"What's that mean?"

"It affected my mental state. And obviously my physical state."

"The stew caused the metamorphosis?"

"Yes."

"Damn."

"The only person in that house was the woman. It was always quiet. I heard her speaking on the phone to a medicine man in Mexico a few times. He apparently put together the concoction and introduced her to those wolf men, who are called 'diableros.' But I couldn't understand most of what she was saying because they spoke mainly Spanish."

"Darn," Anthony said.

"I was famished when she gave me the stew so I nearly inhaled it."

"What was in the stew?"

"I could identify chili peppers, meat of some kind, cactus strips, jalapeños; it was hot and bitter. I was starving, so I swallowed it. Probably the only time in my life I will ever hear the phrase 'wolf afterbirth.' That may have been one of the ingredients, too."

"Dude, that's disgusting."

"I felt like I was getting sick, then my mind started flying. Hours of hallucinations, like I was being torn apart from the inside, my face distorting, my hands distorting. Felt like a tornado inside me. Just glad I made it out alive."

"How did you put that note on my door?"

"After I ate the stew, my spirit started traveling somehow. Once I calmed down, I could direct my exploration. My body was going through those strange mutations, and my spirit moved through space and time and could influence the material world. My physical body was still in the attic, but my ethereal body could travel and influence that environment. So I left you that note."

"Weird."

"Want to hear something really weird?"

"Weirder than this shit?"

"Another spirit protected me. A Mexican man wearing sandals that laced up around his ankles, a hat with colored feathers in the brim, a white cotton shirt with purple designs embroidered on the shoulders, white cotton pants with purple embroidery at the heels, and a colorful little pouch that he carried with a slender rope around his shoulder. The rope was around his left shoulder and the pouch hung next to his right hip. He helped me get you that note. I wanted you to know I was alive."

"Could he speak to you?"

"He knew my thoughts and I could understand his."

"That is some seriously crazy stuff. I don't recommend smoking weed for a while," Anthony joked.

"I'm not going to smoke. I spend every waking moment trying to become grounded, trying to connect myself to my old life. At the same time, I'm accepting the reality that my old life is gone forever. I'm a fifteen-year-old sophomore in high school, who is capable of who knows what."

"Did you say anything to your mom and dad?"

"Yeah, sure. Hey mom and dad, I transformed into one of those wolves and tore some guy's neck off because he was going to shoot Anthony. My dad asked me today if I wanted to go to counseling. Counseling? I want my old life back! I want to go back to simplemindedly hanging at Ottie's and arguing with you about Pearl Jam or Trippie Redd."

"Am I the only one who knows?"

"You are the only one who is ever going to know, Anthony. Our friendship is going to be put to the test. Don't ever text me or put anything in writing about any of this. I don't know where this is going. Best that no one can connect any of it with you."

"Nothing's changed between us. We're right back where we left off."

"I need you, Anthony."

"You got me, dude."

"I'm scared."

"You're way braver than I am. Can you morph into a wolf any time you want?"

"I don't know. I can't exactly practice, can I? I became enraged when I saw that guy point a gun at you in Philadelphia. I'm wondering, do I have to be enraged for this transformation to occur? And what if I become enraged at something at school or at home? Imagine if I began to transform in front of people in a public space! If they kill the wolf, they kill me, Renee. I might have to go to Mexico to find the medicine man. Maybe he can reverse the process."

"Whatever you decide, I'm with you."

"I'm vulnerable. And not sure who I am."

"You'll figure it out, Renee. At the prayer service for you, one of the guidance counselors said you're a genius. You're probably the first wolf in history who is a genius."

"I have one ally—you. That's the scariest part," she said, laughing.

Chapter Twenty-Four

The first weeks of school provided plenty of excitement in Gloucester. The football, field hockey, and girls soccer teams started the season with a string of victories. Gloucester High was cited by a national news magazine as one of ten New Jersey high schools "On the Rise" for the dramatic increase in students taking Advanced Placement classes. In the city, the youth league football fields were dedicated to a courageous former Lions football star who had been killed in action in Iraq, Marine Cpl. Marc Ryan. Summer weather reappeared and enticed people to swim in backyard pools well into October, mocking autumn lovers who put up Halloween decorations in mid-September. Renee attended full days of school beginning on September 11 and returned immediately to smartest-kid-in-the-class mode. Teachers and students were deferential and compassionate. The accepted wisdom in Gloucester was that Renee had been kidnapped by a woman who forced her to wear a suicide bomb in a desperate attempt to free a drug cartel leader from prison. Nobody asked any questions.

The national news was dominated by fear of a nuclear war, football players "taking a knee," and tropical storm damage in U.S. territories. Local news watchers were appalled by a series of assaults on female joggers in Fairmount Park in Philadelphia.

Fairmount Park is the largest landscaped urban park in the world. Located on 9,600 acres in the heart of Philadelphia, Fairmount Park contains the country's oldest zoo and a ten-mile stretch of wooded paths where vehicular traffic is forbidden. Forbidden Drive Trail is popular year-round for jogging, biking, and walking. In late September, vicious, premeditated attacks on joggers shook the community. A White male in grey sweatpants and a red hoodie threw a corrosive liquid onto the faces of young women in two separate attacks. He escaped into the woods each time and was not apprehended. The attacks were physically disfiguring, and reporters speculated that victims could experience long-term social and economic difficulties.

After school ended on Wednesday, October 4, Renee took an Uber to Fairmount Park. The driver delivered her to the Philadelphia Museum of Art. The park was buzzing with dynamic motion. Runners pushed strollers. Senior citizens rode recumbent bicycles. Roller bladers, walkers, college cross-country teams, and twelve-minute-a-mile joggers enjoyed the beautiful October sunshine, with earbuds in place and music streaming.

Renee walked up the west side of the river toward the zoo. How would she signal her body that she wanted to transform? Would she have to hide her clothes? What if she got close to a target and the transformation didn't occur? Dusk was approaching. Renee wrapped her phone inside her hoodie and hid it beneath a sculpture of a limestone Indian sitting amidst swaths of deep green vegetation. She walked through the woods on the edge of the trail and struggled to maintain her focus on searching for the attacker. She moved with a newfound grace, so stealthy in her gait that she felt invisible. Her metamorphosis was a slow, staggered process. Her senses became keener, seeing clearly through the dusk, detecting motion a quarter mile away, hearing the soft creak of tree limbs blowing in the autumn winds. She began to run. She ran so fast that the physical world blurred, and she depended on sensual reality to guide her. When she saw a man in a red hoodie twist the lid off a steel container and cock his arm back near a lone jogger, a frenzied, angry efficiency of instincts overcame her. It lasted twenty seconds.

She returned to the dullness of her thinking senses while washing off in a bathroom near the arboretum, splashing cold water into her eyes and face. She found her phone and hoodie and returned to leave a calling card at the scene. She had decided to leave a mark she hoped would distinguish her from the diableros. She rode back to Gloucester, glancing at her phone on the way: twenty-five texts, sixteen missed calls.

She texted Anthony:

"Hey, can you meet me at Ottie's in fifteen minutes?"

"Ottie's closed an hour ago, dude. Where have you been? Your parents are freaking."

"Snap. I lost all concept of time. My poor parents."

"Text them and tell them you're all right."

"I'll just go home. See you tomorrow at school."

"You okay?"

"I guess so. We gotta talk. Can we meet before school in the Media Center? It opens at seven thirty. Can you get up that early?"

"Yeah. Meet you in the Media Center at the back tables at seven-thirty. Good luck with your parents, dude."

"I'll need it."

Renee asked the driver to drop her off at the swim club parking lot and walked down Brown Street, normally the most bucolic expanse of the city but reduced since June to a dusty construction site as the city replaced water and sewer pipes. She turned to her house on Chambers Avenue and felt dread in her belly as she walked up the steps, caught between the new truth of serving as an avenging spirit and the continuing truth of living with parents who had reasonable expectations of safety, trust, and honesty.

"Renee, this is totally unacceptable," her mother said. "Where on earth have you been? It's nearly eleven o'clock on a school night! No phone call! No text! Anthony didn't have any idea where you were. Your friends from band had no idea where you were. After everything we've been through this summer, it's irresponsible and callous of you."

"I'm really sorry. I'm dealing with the aftermath of the summer. It's overwhelming and confusing. I'm extremely sorry and I apologize. I'll try to never let it happen again," Renee said.

"You didn't 'let' it happen," her father said "You made it happen. Another serious error in judgment."

"That's how you've processed what I endure this summer, as an error in judgment?"

The television droned in the background with talking heads bickering about gun control.

"Make a commitment to see a psychiatrist, Renee," her father insisted. "You have post-traumatic stress disorder. How couldn't you? Let's be allies on this. Please. Your mother and I are going to go to seek counseling, too. We've all been through hell. You leaving school at three and returning home at ten thirty is the final straw. We've been worried sick."

Renee's mother grabbed the television remote and raised the volume.

"Breaking news from Fairmount Park tonight. A twenty-five-year-old man holding a steel container of nitric acid was found badly mauled this evening in a remote area of Forbidden Drive. Police are investigating whether his wounds are similar to wounds inflicted during this summer's wolf attacks in Philadelphia and

Gloucester City."

Renee's mother began to cry.

"Can you believe there might still be wolves around?" she said.

"I thought the cops said they had all been killed," her dad said.

The newscaster continued, "The victim is considered to be the prime suspect in the sadistic attacks on female joggers in Fairmount Park. Eyewitnesses tell ABC News that his head was nearly severed. An origami bird had been placed in his eye socket with the message, 'What's a goon to a goblin?'"

Her mother sobbed. Her father sat with his head in his hands, and Renee said, "I'm going to get a shower. I have school tomorrow."

Chapter Twenty-Five

The next morning, Renee walked to the back on the Media Center and sat with Anthony at a secluded table. Anthony opened a *Philadelphia Daily News* he had purchased at Wawa. The front page headline glared:

"What's a Goon to a Goblin?"

The headline hovered over a rendering of a timber wolf and the story of the acid attacker being slain last evening.

"I'm assuming you hung out in Fairmount Park last night. The Lil Wayne lyric is a nice touch," Anthony said.

"Anthony, I killed someone last night."

"A psycho who was going to keep ruining women's lives until somebody stopped him? You stopped him," Anthony replied.

"Big disconnect between attending high school during the day and tearing people apart at night," Renee said.

"Especially for you," Anthony said. "You're so gentle."

"It's creating cognitive dissonance," Renee said.

"Like a headache?"

"My behavior is not consistent with my beliefs."

"What you did last night was great. Know how long it might have taken the

Philadelphia police to nab that guy? Fairmount Park is bigger than Gloucester.

That guy might have ruined ten more lives. You put him out of commission,"

Anthony said.

"Makes me uncomfortable just thinking about it."

"Must not have worried you last night."

"Everything anyone does seems like a good idea until it seems like a bad idea,"

Renee said.

"Maybe I'll write a book one day called *The History of Horrendous Ideas*,"

Anthony said.

"It would be hundreds of volumes," Renee replied.

"Are you getting the hang of going 'Beast Mode?'"

"It's more like I allow it to happen. Stop my thoughts and accept the changes."

"Very mystical."

"Why me?"

"Who better than you? Should I wait for you to walk home from school?"

"Yes, please. I have to go right home for a while to regain my parent's

confidence. They were ready to have me committed last night," Renee said.

"Meet you in front of the auditorium at three o'clock," Anthony said.

"Have fun."

"I always have fun, Renee. Otherwise I'd stop coming."

After a day examining pathos and parallelism, contextualizing historical evidence, reading Chaucer, and studying alterations of the Earth's surface, the two fifteen-year-olds walked home.

"Have my facial features changed?" Renee asked.

"Honestly, you're prettier than ever," Anthony said.

"Feel free to give me status updates. I'm afraid of turning into a wolf girl or something."

"Was it cool using your wolf sense to track that psycho?"

"I've become clairvoyant. I had a premonition after school that something was going to happen in Fairmount Park last evening. That's why I went. I just knew. I knew what his plans were and intercepted him."

"You're clairvoyant?"

"I think so. I can intuit people's intentions since the ordeal. I sense stuff before it happens. Still getting used to it. Still trying to figure it out."

"It's cool you're sharing this with me," Anthony said.

"I share everything with you. Let's talk about normal stuff. Are you keeping your intention to do better in school this year?"

"Of course not. The road to hell is paved with good intentions. Already driving half my teachers nuts. I've cooled off a little, I guess, considering how I used to be. Haven't gotten sent to the office yet."

"Must have some patient teachers."

As they walked around Martin's Lake and up East Brown, their fingers touched, just the outside at first, and then the fingertips, and then their fingers joined. Neither said a word and they quickly arrived at Renee's house.

"I have to stay in tonight," Renee said. "I'll see you tomorrow in school."

Anthony exhaled loudly.

"I'll text you later," he said.

"Great."

Anthony texted her as soon as he got to Ottie's.

"Dude, my mind took off like a rocket ship when our hands touched. Never felt that sensation before. I was soaring."

"I was thrilled," Renee replied. "We tiptoed around it for a long while."

"That was my stupid fault. Always felt way closer to you than anyone I've ever known," Anthony said.

"You tend to get super enthused about anything new."

"I've been super enthused about you all summer."

"Let's see where it goes," Renee said.

"Okay, I'll text you later."

"Thanks for being you, Anthony."

Chapter Twenty-Six

After walking uphill through the first six weeks of the school year, students caught their breath during the long Columbus Day weekend. Renee and Anthony met at Ottie's at noon on Monday.

"Are things starting to get better with your parents?" Anthony asked.

"Back to normal, almost. They're attributing my new eccentricities to post-traumatic stress. I don't know how I'm going to handle the whole dynamic going forward. I can't tell them about the transmutation because they'll freak out and insist I seek medical treatment to have it reversed. I'd be seeing specialists from here to Missouri."

"Still thinking about looking for the medicine man in Mexico?"

"I've been thinking about it and I can't decide whether I want to reverse it. It has its benefits and its dangers."

"The danger in this case is death," Anthony said.

"The danger of riding a motorcycle without a helmet is death. The danger of climbing mountains is death. The danger of a guy getting into a boxing ring is death. The danger of being in the Marines is death. Death's a constant companion for many people."

"And the benefits?"

"Protecting the innocent."

"Or avenging the innocent," Anthony said.

"That Mexican cop almost killed you solely because you could connect him to Ana. Good thing I was there to protect you."

"I've been thinking about that. I was an inch away from getting blasted. If you weren't at Jerome's, I wouldn't even be here now."

"Jerome might have shot him."

"Or he might not have."

"Glad I was able to handle it. I want to be able to help other people, too."

"Well, you've got plenty of those origami birds to leave as your calling card," Anthony joked.

"The tough part is going to be doing it within the parameters my parents set and going to high school and being a normal teenager," Renee said.

"Speaking of being a normal teenager, do you want to go to the Homecoming Dance with me?" Anthony asked.

"Yes, that will be nice."

"I was going to spell it out in Orange Fanta soda cans. I was afraid you wouldn't see the humor in it."

"I miss those carefree nights. Now everything feels heavy and serious."

"You can always start smoking again."

148

"No, I can't. This is crazy enough when I'm clearheaded."

"I'll smoke enough for both of us. I need it for my PTSD," Anthony said.

"I need you, Anthony. Please don't regress."

"You're asking for a lot," he said.

"Thank you for everything you did. You put your life on the line for me."

"Dude, when I got that note from you, it felt like my heart collapsed. I couldn't breathe."

"Autonomic nervous system going haywire, glands over-functioning, adrenaline release in max capacity, all involuntary processes triggered by deep emotions," Renee said.

"You go to med school when you were missing?"

"I paid attention in biology class."

"Had a feeling I was missing something."

"Should have stayed awake. What I want to know is why the deep emotionality? Huh, Anthony?"

"That's when I first realized I liked you maybe more than just as a friend."

"And...?"

"And here we are," he said.

"Here we are, two buddies hanging out on Columbus Day?"

"More than just buddies, I hope."

"I am trusting you with so much," Renee said.

"Already proved how much you mean to me," Anthony replied.

"Think it over before you get in any deeper. It's so much to ask of someone. I have mixed feelings about drawing you into all of this," Renee said.

"Already thought about it. I'm all in," Anthony said.

"Still have the money from Jerome?"

"How's this for a cliché? It's under my mattress."

"I want you to keep my part of it."

"No way, dude. You earned it with everything you went through."

"If anything ever happens to me, it's yours."

"Don't want to think about that."

"And if anything doesn't happen to me, it's yours. My family provides for me. You've been on your own since the day I met you."

"My mom keeps in touch. We talk every day."

"Keeps in touch? She's supposed to be nurturing you and protecting you."

"There's benefits to her parenting style," Anthony said.

"That's an enormous rationalization. The money is yours. All of it."

"Should have asked you to the Homecoming sooner," Anthony joked.

"When is the Homecoming Dance?"

"You go to the school and you don't know when anything is," Anthony said.

"I know where my classes are," Renee replied.

"The Homecoming Dance is the last Saturday in October. We play Pennsville in football on Friday and the dance is Saturday."

"That's right. I remember last year we decorated the hallways at night. Don't remember seeing you there, by the way."

"I was doing homework."

"You haven't done homework since second grade."

"Give me some credit. I did it for two years."

"You know how smart you could be if you ever worked?"

"My uncle is taking me to see the Sixers practice facility in Camden this afternoon. Want to go with me?"

"I'll pass, but thanks anyway. I have stuff to do. Hope you have fun," Renee said.

"Want me to come over when I get back?

"Sure. See you tonight."

Chapter Twenty-Seven

Anthony walked to Renee's at six o'clock. They sat on her front steps and talked.

"How'd you like the new Sixers practice facility?" Renee asked.

"It was so cool. None of the players were around, but we got a nice tour of the building. And they let us shoot hoops on the new court for about fifteen minutes. Just thinking I was shooting at the same basket as Ben Simmons was getting me pumped. My uncle bought a ten-game ticket package, and a tour of the new practice facility was included. It was fun," Anthony said.

"Nice of your uncle to take you."

"He's my mom's brother. Think he feels bad because she's not around much and I don't have a dad. He says he's going to take me to a couple of games with him. What'd you do all day?"

"I took an Uber to Wharton State Forest after you left. I'm exploring the parameters of my new powers. I wanted to flex my muscles a little bit and try to gain some understanding of my new potential. Wish there was a Hogwarts for freshly minted wolves."

"What did you find out?"

"I'm stealthy. I walked so close to these hikers and they didn't notice me."

"Good thing they didn't. You might have given one of them a heart attack."

"Might have given myself heart attack if they saw me. Wolves aren't supposed to be in New Jersey, remember?"

"Bet a lot of kids in Gloucester are gonna be wolves for Halloween this year?"

"Maybe I'll transform and roam around town with a trick-or-treat bag hanging from my mouth," Renee said.

"Sounds like you're thinking about maintaining your new abilities rather than searching for the shaman to change you back to your old self."

"I'm conflicted. One minute I want to go back to my former self, and the next minute I can't wait to try out some new powers."

A sweeping breeze made the inflatable witches, cotton spider webs, and plastic ghosts sway on the porch behind them.

"Something unsettling happened in Philadelphia last night," Renee said. "I saw it online when I came home today. Let me show you." Renee scrolled through her phone until she found the story. "Look at this."

"'Double homicide in West Philly,'" Anthony read aloud. "'Police discovered two bodies inside the former Mr. Silk's Third Base Lounge on 52nd Street in West Philadelphia. Police have yet to release the identities of the victims. The victims appear to have been tortured.' Damn!"

"Hope it wasn't anyone we know," Renee replied.

"I thought Jerome and Yvonne were going to stay away for a while," Anthony said.

"Hope so. The police will release the victims' names at some point."

"Really hope it wasn't those guys," Anthony said.

"Really hope it wasn't connected to the ordeal this summer," Renee said.

"You think it could be?"

"Possibly. It's logical. Three million bucks is a lot of money."

"The cartel probably has a billion dollars."

"Could be revenge for Ana's death," Renee said.

"Hope they ain't looking for us," Anthony said.

"They don't know about us," Renee insisted.

"They know about you. You're famous. All they'd have to do is read stuff on the internet," Anthony said. "They'd know you're the girl Ana kidnapped. If anyone's seeking revenge, it's probably Ana's brother's crew."

"Thanks for the positive outlook," Renee said.

"I'll be your bodyguard."

"What would you do, smash a pumpkin on them?"

"It probably ain't got nothing to do with the stuff this summer. I bet Jerome is a major player over in Philly. You just don't come up with all those crazy weapons if you're just a guy opening a bar. He's always got a gun and knife on him. And the way he took charge that day in the parking lot? Kept his cool like he'd been through stuff like that before."

"You're right. We shouldn't let our imaginations run wild."

A Gloucester police car pulled up. It was Detective O'Brien.

"Renee, you're in bad company tonight. Thought people tell me you're real smart. You're not still hanging with this hammer, are you?" O'Brien asked.

"Handsomest kid in Gloucester High. She couldn't resist," Anthony said.

"That school's been going downhill since I left," O'Brien said. "When I pulled up, I thought you were a trick or treater. Then I remembered Halloween's not until another couple of weeks."

O'Brien shook Anthony's hand.

"Good to see you, Anthony. And from another perspective, glad to see you have the good sense to stick with somebody smart and goodhearted," O'Brien said, nodding at Renee.

"Renee, can we go inside? I have to speak with you and your parents. Are they home?"

"Yes."

"Anthony, gonna have to send you on your way, buddy. This might take a while. Aren't the Sixers playing tonight?"

"Yeah. They're playing the Celtics. I was at their new practice facility this afternoon with my uncle. Even got to shoot on the court for a while."

"Did you break into the new facility, or did you get invited?"

"You're hilarious, dude."

"Good seeing you, Anthony," O'Brien said. "Keep doing the right thing, buddy."

"Yeah, good seeing you."

Renee led O'Brien into her home and sat down with her mom and dad.

"Hello, again, Mr. and Mrs. Sears. We might still be dealing with the consequences of the trouble from the summer. Something alarming happened this afternoon and I want to talk with you about it. It's best we err on the side of caution, I think."

"Something else has happened?" Renee's mom asked.

"Tangentially, yes. There was a double homicide in Philadelphia yesterday that looks like it could be related to the problems from summer," O'Brien said. "Took place in a bar in West Philadelphia known as Mr. Silk's Third Base Lounge. The victims are thought to be participants in the shootout on that side of the bridge. In August, Philadelphia police found a shell casing at the parking lot where the woman who kidnapped Renee was killed. The casing had one of the homicide victim's fingerprints on it. Now he shows up tortured and dead. Could be a revenge killing."

"Was one of the deceased named Jerome?" Renee asked.

"Don't think the Philadelphia PD has released the names yet," O'Brien said. "Why do you ask?"

"Oh, nothing. I vaguely remember a man named Jerome coming to my assistance at one point, that's all. I hope he wasn't at the bar."

O'Brien looked baffled.

"You can imagine how traumatized Renee has been by her ordeal, Detective. We're hoping she'll begin receiving therapy for post-traumatic stress. My own therapist told me that her mind may be shutting off certain memories until she's healed enough to process them," Mrs. Sears said.

"I'm sorry to hear that, Renee. You're such a strong person. The reason I'm here is because two guys came into the Gloucester Wawa this afternoon and offered the clerk a hundred dollars if she could tell them where you live."

Mrs. Sears gasped. "She didn't take the money, did she?"

"Well, being it's Gloucester, she did take the money. But she sent them down to Charles Street and called us. We sent three squad cars down but didn't find them. They might be waiting until after dark."

"What could they want with a fifteen-year-old girl?" Renee's father asked.

"Your guess is as good as mine, sir," O'Brien said. "We would like to station a police officer outside your house until we get a handle on this."

"Yes, that would be great," Mrs. Sears said.

"No, mom, it wouldn't be great. It would make me more of a freak than I already am. I can handle this myself," Renee said.

"Who says you're a freak, Renee?" her father asked.

"How many fifteen-year-olds were kidnapped, starved, made to wear an explosive vest, and who knows what else?" Renee asked.

"I'm sorry, honey, but it's for your own protection," her mom insisted.

"So we'll have a police officer out front 'round the clock," O'Brien said.

"We're very grateful, detective," Renee's dad said.

"Here's my cell number. Call me any time. Renee, you're as brave as anyone I've ever known. I'm sorry about all this," O'Brien said. He shook her parents' hands and left.

"Can I go see Anthony?" Renee asked.

"He can come back over here," her dad suggested.

"That was quick. I just was walking up my steps when you texted to come back," Anthony said when he arrived.

"They think the guys who killed the people at Mr. Silk's came to Gloucester afterwards and were offering people money to find out where I live."

"Holy shit! Where are they now?"

"Who knows? A police officer will be guarding my house twenty-four hours a day."

"Good thing."

"No, it's a bad thing. I want to find the guys. They came here to teach Jerome a lesson. I'm going to teach them a lesson."

"What's the lesson?" Anthony asked.

"Don't mess with Renee Sears."

"Dude, are you taking steroids?"

"I haven't told you certain things because I'm still wrapping my mind around all the changes. Remember I said I was walking near the hikers this afternoon and they couldn't see me?"

"Yeah."

"Anthony, I was walking right between them, brushing against them, and they couldn't even see me."

"You were invisible?"

"I don't know. It's not like there's a guidebook. But those wolves we saw at the ballfields? I'm them to the hundredth power. I was running super fast in the woods today and I felt strong—really strong. Unless you're on a Ducati motorcycle, you're not catching me."

"Don't go crazy. You're the one always telling me to stay grounded," Anthony said.

"After my parents go to bed, I'm going to find those guys and eliminate them."

Chapter Twenty-Eight

The police found that Renee's house was a challenge to protect. It was half-swallowed by vegetation. Her parents lived cerebral, introspective lives, keenly aware of their thoughts and feelings but often blind to the growth, decay, and movement of the natural world. It was not uncommon for either of her parents to run out of gas while driving or to lock themselves out of their house. A neighbor once asked them if they had received any insurance estimates yet for the disintegrating foundation of their garage. They hadn't even noticed it. Unruly shrubbery grabbed the wrought iron railing on the left side of the front porch. Evergreen and azalea bushes arm-wrestled on the right side. Three massive thirty-foot pines stood sentinel on the right forefront, obscuring the view of their side porch. The only way to see the right side of the house was to peek beneath the conifers. They paid a guy to mow the lawn, but no other vegetation had been pruned since the Sears family moved to Gloucester eight years ago. Greenery obscured everything but the front steps. A police officer parked the squad car at the curb twenty feet from the front steps. It was the only space that offered an unobstructed view of the front door.

Renee waited until midnight to ensure that her parents were deep in slumber, slipped on her size 6 Mizuno Wave Riders, and crept down the stairs, through the kitchen and out the back door. She closed the door in slow motion behind her, catapulted over the fence, and jogged to Johnson Boulevard. She crossed the railroad tracks, hid her clothing behind the Marc Ryan monument, and transformed. She ran along the railroad tracks and climbed the hill at the Water Works to avoid the lights at the public basketball courts. She turned onto the 900 block of Bergen, seeking a shroud of darkness. Unsure of her visibility, she remained cautious and circumspect. She searched from Bergen to Essex Street and found no strange vehicles, strange people, or signs of surveillance. Frustrated, she traveled back to the monument, transformed, got dressed, and headed home. The most challenging part of the night's excursion was crawling through her back yard and entering the back door without disturbing the police officer out front.

On Tuesday morning, Renee awoke as she did every morning, to the sound of her cell phone playing Cardi B's "Bodak Yellow." She slid off her bed onto her knees, whispered a short prayer, and stood stretching her fingers toward her ceiling. She showered, dressed, and greeted her parents at the breakfast table. After enjoying two pieces of toast with almond butter, she kissed her mom and dad goodbye and walked to school. By mid-October, Renee's school day began at seven thirty. She participated in concert band practice or choir rehearsal on alternating days. Music practices before school allowed musicians and singers to take part in school sports or club activities after school. Renee belonged to the

Graphic Novel Club, Student Council, the Yoga Club, the STEM Club, and Friends of Rachel, a service organization. She walked toward the high school, lugging her backpack and her flute case, debating whether she should participate in the upcoming dramatic presentation, *The Prince and The Pea*. Renee was a rising star in the school's musical productions but had little enthusiasm for straight drama. She scampered over the crabgrass along Martin's Lake and turned down Highland Boulevard alongside the Minnow Hole, ducking under overgrown shrub branches wet with dew. The Minnow Hole has two wooden fishing docks; two men stood fishing, one on each dock. As Renee walked past the first dock, the fisherman yelled, in a muddy Texas accent:

"Hey, is there bass in this lake?"

"I'm not sure," Renee replied. "I don't fish."

When she turned her head around to continue her path to the high school, the second fisherman was blocking the sidewalk. His hands were in the front pocket of a grey hoodie and he jabbed what felt like the tip of a gun into Renee's ribs. The front of his hoodie said, "Don't Mess With Texas."

"See that brown van? Walk over and get into the back like you just ran into your uncle and he offered your ride to school. If you run, I'll shoot you."

The first man gathered the fishing gear, and the men shepherded Renee into the van. The back of the van was windowless and had no seats. Renee sat on her backpack to avoid the rust on the floor of the van. They sped down Greenwood and within ninety seconds were moving across the Walt Whitman Bridge. When they exited the bridge, Renee caught quick glimpses of Vietnamese restaurants, tile outlets, Mexican groceries, and pawn shops in angled glances out the front windshield. She knew she was in South Philadelphia. Renee had traveled these streets many times on the way to her parents' favorite store, Molly's Books & Records. Her father collected vinyl records and her mom collected first-edition vintage cookbooks.

Renee was patient, ready to settle the score with everyone involved with this enterprise once and for all. The van stopped at a defunct carpet outlet in the no-man's land between Washington and Grey's Ferry Avenues. The men grabbed her roughly by her upper arms and led her through a side door into an office that abutted a large empty warehouse. She carried the strap of her backpack in one hand and her flute case in the other. Three well-dressed men were leaning against faded green filing cabinets in the office area. A large flat-topped desk, a swivel chair, and three flat-backed wooden chairs were arranged in a circle in the room.

"You must be Renee," one of the men said.

"Yes," she said, breathing calmly.

One of the fishermen said, "We got you a day off from school. You oughta thank us."

164

"I like school. I want to be back by lunch," Renee replied.

"Answer our questions honestly and you'll be back by lunch, I promise," a well-dressed man said. "Take a seat."

Renee sat in one of the wooden chairs. "What questions?" she asked.

"I'm calling a friend of ours in Mexico City. He is a cousin of Ana, the woman you met at the end of the summer. He's got a few questions for you."

"I didn't 'meet' Ana. She kidnapped me. That's how we 'met.'"

"He and Ana were very close. He wants to ask you what happened."

Renee bided her time. The phone connection went through, and the well-dressed man placed a cell phone on top of two thick telephone books from another century that were sitting on the desk. He put the phone on speaker.

"Renee is here," he said to his boss in Mexico City. "She's ready to answer your questions."

"Renee, I understand you spent some time with my cousin, Ana."

"She kidnapped me. She wanted me to wear an explosive vest to blow myself up so that her brother could escape. She was a coldhearted bitch."

"What happened at to Ana, Renee? She was cautious and conservative. Never reckless. Never anything but diligent. Someone betrayed her and we want to know who. If you tell us the truth, we will release you unharmed. Understand?"

"I hear what you're saying," Renee replied.

"So what happened?" he asked.

"Ana committed suicide when she realized the plan was foiled. She blew herself up," Renee said.

"I take great offense at that, Renee. Every lie from here on costs you a finger," he said.

"Tell the truth and you may live to see an old age. That is my fervent wish for you."

One of the fishermen retrieved a large pair of wire cutters from his tackle box, glared at Renee, and squeezed them.

"I'm telling you the truth, sir. Ana purchased an explosive vest from a man from New York. She made me wear it. She held the detonator in her hand. When she realized she had been double-crossed, she released the detonator and killed herself."

"Two concerns: why didn't you get blown up along with her if you were wearing the vest? And you are going to give me the name of the person who double crossed her or we will kill you. Am I making myself clear?"

"Yes, and I will explain, sir, but can I please go to the bathroom? I'm fifteen-years-old and I'm scared."

"Take her to the bathroom and wait outside the door. Bring her right back."

One of the fishermen caressed the wire cutters and the other walked with her

166

until they found a bathroom at the end of the warehouse.

"Be quick," he said.

Renee transformed but couldn't open the bathroom door to get back out. She rammed into the door three times and the fisherman opened it.

"What the hell are you doing?" he said. Those were his final words.

On the way back to the office, she passed one of the well-dressed men smoking a cigarette and killed him silently. She entered the office and attacked. The fisherman pulled a handgun out of the tackle box but was dead before he could pull the trigger. The battle took twenty seconds. She could hear the voice of the man in Mexico demanding to know what was going on. Renee went back into the bathroom, got dressed, and came back to the office. The cell phone connection had gone dead. She grabbed the phone from the top of the telephone books and walked through the carpet warehouse, filming the dead kidnappers. She looked at the phone's list of recent calls, placed the number from Mexico into a text message box, attached the video, and transmitted it to the man in Mexico City. She powered off the phone and slid it into her pocket. She contacted Uber from her phone and arranged to be picked up in front of the Mummer's Museum. Before leaving, she took five origami birds from the collection in her backpack and placed one on each of her captors' bodies with a note reading,

"What's a goon to a goblin?"

Chapter Twenty-Nine

Renee arrived at school just after lunch. As she signed in at the front office, she saw the silhouettes of her parents through the door to the vice principal's office. The school secretary Ms. Nevins said, "Hi, Renee. Glad to see you. People have been worried because you didn't come to school. Your parents are with Ms. Kelly. I'll let everyone know you're here."

I'm in a no-win situation, Renee thought. I'll just sit down and be humble, like the song says. That's the only card I can play here.

As crazy as it seemed, she had to face the consequences of "skipping school" that morning. Seconds later, she sensed her parents approaching. Her mom was crying when they hugged, and her father felt feverish through his shirt when she hugged him. As he held her, she heard his muffled cry. She deeply regretted that her difficulties were altering their relationship. If they only knew the half of it, she thought. Ms. Kelly, the vice principal, stood behind them and spoke.

"How about we sit down in my office and talk, Renee?"

"Sure."

Ms. Kelly held out her arm and gestured for everyone to enter her office, then closed the door.

"Renee, as I'm sure you can understand, your parents were frantic when we told them you didn't arrive at school this morning."

"I do understand, and I'm sorry."

"Renee, you've had to apologize for more behavior in the past month than in the previous fifteen years," her mom added.

"I'm sorry, Mom. It's all related to the trauma at the end of the summer. I'm dealing with so much. I don't think I could make you understand even if I tried, so there's no sense trying. All of this has been thrust upon me. I didn't volunteer for any of it. And please don't counter that I shouldn't have been naive enough to take a closer look at the wolves. It wasn't wolves who hurt me. It was a human."

"Why can't you explain to us just a little of what you're going through?"

"I can't get a grasp on it myself, Mom. Things shift every day. A police officer is permanently stationed outside our house. How many fifteen-year-olds are under twenty-four hour police watch?"

Ms. Kelly cleared her throat.

"Renee, the school is concerned for your welfare and well-being. You are one of the superstars of our building. It pains me to see you struggle. It pains me to see caring, loving parents so heartbroken. I'm going to insist that you receive counseling. I'm not going to administer any discipline for cutting school this morning, but I want you to assure me that you're willing to engage in a therapeutic conversation with someone."

"It will be completely confidential, Renee," her father added. "I give you my word that your mother and I will not pry. We won't ask you about what is transpiring in therapy and we will not ask the therapist."

"I'll have to have a good feeling about whomever I'm going to speak with," Renee said. "I can't trust just anybody."

"We'll research who the most respected adolescent therapists in this area are, and you can choose which one you want to see. If you don't feel comfortable, we will move on until you find someone you trust. Nothing changes if nothing changes. Something has to change because our family is in turmoil."

"Ok, I'll see someone."

"You won't regret it, Renee. Can you keep a secret?" Ms. Kelly asked.

"I'm keeping a lot of secrets," Renee said.

"Can you keep one more?"

"I'm almost out of room, but I'll squeeze one more in for you, Ms. Kelly."

"I've seen a therapist for the past few years, trying to make sense of events from my own childhood. Since I began therapy, I sleep better, my spirit feels lighter, and I've been able to release a good deal of anger and resentment. It's been life-changing."

"Sign me up then, please," Renee said, "because I've been walking through a nightmare these past six weeks. My spirit is in turmoil. I want to go back to having

170

a normal life. Am I allowed to go to my seventh and eighth period classes?"

"Yes. Ms. Nevins will give you a note. Make the most of your afternoon."

Renee thanked Ms. Kelly, hugged her mom and dad, and headed to class. Her mind raced. Should she tell Anthony about this morning's craziness? Can she really be open and honest with a therapist? Is this the life she wants?

As soon as school ended, she found Anthony.

"Want to go to Ottie's?" Renee asked.

"Thought you had a club activity on Tuesday?" Anthony asked.

"Not in the mood for the Graphic Novel Club. I feel like I'm living inside a graphic novel. I better text my mom:

'Okay if I talk to Anthony for a while? I have my phone on so call or text me if you need me. I'll be home at 5:30. I am very, very sorry about this morning, Mom. I love you with all my heart.'"

They walked out the front doors onto Market Street. Her phone buzzed.

"Trusting you to do the right thing, Renee. Please don't be late. And I think you should plan to stay in tonight. I love you always."

"Where were you this morning?" Anthony asked. "Ms. Kelly called me down and asked if I knew where you were."

"I saw your texts. I apologize. My morning was insane. And it's crazy that every time I don't do what I'm supposed to, people assume you have something to do with it," she said.

"It's my karma, dude. What happened this morning?" Anthony asked.

"I'm pleading the fifth. Let's get back to our old friendship. I feel like I've made you my confessor. I want to be friends again. I promised my parents and Ms. Kelly that I'll see a therapist. I'm sure my mom is compiling a list from Yelp recommendations right now. I want us to get back to the ease we use to have."

"Before you needed twenty-four hour police protection?"

"Earlier."

"Before your rampage in Fairmount Park?"

"Earlier."

"Before you offed that crooked cop?"

"Earlier."

"Before you ate the magic stew?"

"Earlier."

"Before we saw the wolves?"

"Yes. Let's go back to how relaxed we were around each other before we saw the wolves."

"Sounds good to me, dude."

Renee switched her flute case to her left hand so she could hold Anthony's with her right. They were passing Martin's Lake.

"Eight hours ago, I was innocently walking right by here on my way to concert band practice and then…."

"And then what?"

"Forget it. Let's talk about Kendrick Lamar or Meek Mill."

"Want to walk to my house instead of Ottie's?"

"Okay, but I have to be home by five thirty. Definitely have to comply with my parents' wishes. I've put them through so much. I feel terrible about it."

"We can just chill."

They arrived at Anthony's, put their backpacks down, and sat on his couch. Anthony streamed Pandora's Metallica station through his sound bar.

"You're not thinking of trying to seduce me to Metallica, are you?" Renee asked.

"I wasn't really sure what we were going to be doing. Sounds like you had a rough morning. Plus, I never really need any mood music, just my charm," Anthony joked.

"And the weed, don't forget. Weed is probably your idea of foreplay," Renee said.

"What do you know about foreplay?" Anthony said, sliding alongside her.

"Not much, sadly, but I know it does not involve 'Enter Sandman.'"

"Am I killing your vibe?"

"It's going to be a tough hurdle to get over, Anthony, because we've never crossed this boundary."

And then they were kissing to "Enter Sandman." After a half hour of cuddling, Anthony walked Renee home. He carried her backpack and she carried her flute case.

"Is my face changing at all?" Renee asked before they left the house.

"I noticed you have whiskers now, but that's the only change I can see," Anthony said.

Renee backhanded his chest. "Don't try to be funny. I'm worried."

"Still worried you might develop wolf characteristics?"

"I'm afraid I might transform one day and not fully transform back."

"When's the last time you transformed?"

"No therapy, remember. Let's just be us."

"Oh, yeah, just two lovers on a distant shore," he replied.

"Star-crossed lovers seeking solace from a cold, uncaring world."

"Sounds like us. Good luck finding a therapist."

"My mom's probably got a list of men therapists, women therapists, Jungians, Freudians, past life guides, you name it. That good woman is thorough and efficient."

"Good luck, dude," Anthony said, handing Renee her backpack. She wrapped it onto her back, put her right hand on his shoulder, and kissed him goodbye.

Chapter Thirty

Anthony started walking Renee to school every morning—a painful pleasure because he watched the Western Conference NBA game each night and didn't get to bed until after midnight and Renee had to be in so early to rehearse with the band and choir.

"Any luck picking a therapist?" he asked groggily. "How did things go when you went home yesterday?"

"I'm worried about confidentiality. Can I really tell a therapist what I've done and trust they won't tell the police? Remember what the guidance counselors said at the beginning of the school year? They said they keep stuff in complete confidence unless we say we are going to hurt ourselves or someone else; then they have to report it."

"Report it to who?"

"Our parents, the police...."

"Do only guidance counselors have to follow that law, or every counselor?"

"I'm assuming every counselor."

"You're not going to hurt yourself. You've got an awesome boyfriend."

"And I'd have every reason to hurt myself after listening to your nonstop basketball chatter."

"Do you really think about hurting yourself?"

"Never. I have hurt other people though."

"Scumbags who were hurting innocent people."

"They'd probably still have to report it. Just to solve a crime or close a case."

Anthony headed to Wawa for some breakfast. Renee went to practice the marching band's rendition of Panic! At The Disco's "Victorious."

Renee had two extracurricular activities after school: Yoga Club and then hallway decorating for Homecoming. Renee cherished Tuesday afternoon yoga practice, taught by a popular art teacher, Ms. Pond. "Remain flexible in mind and body" was the woman's mantra. Renee promised herself she would try. After yoga, she worked with her classmates painting posters to be hung during Spirit Week, when classes competed in an activity each day (who had the most students wearing school colors, who had the best hall decorations, etc.). Renee painted for an hour, retrieved her backpack from her locker, and walked home.

She called Anthony on her cell as she walked down Greenwood. He didn't answer. Probably at the courts playing basketball, she thought. Renee enjoyed seeing the ghosts, witches, corn husks, black cats, and spider webs that adorned houses in anticipation of Halloween. She passed a yard decorated as a cemetery with a sign that read, "How Do You Want to Be Remembered?"

Young boys were casting lines all around both lakes. Renee walked past

Martin's Lake, carefully stepping around the goose poop that dotted the sidewalk, and noticed an old man sitting on a bench beneath a cluster of tall evergreens along Kathryn Street. He was ancient looking with brown weathered skin. His sandals were held to his furrowed feet by strands of dirty twine. He wore a palm straw hat with feathers in the side band and a pouch hanging from a slender rope that was slung over his left shoulder and across his right hip. He stared at Renee with doleful, sad eyes, slowly inhaling on a cigarette and releasing the smoke with a melancholy sigh. An amulet on a worn and beaten leather strap, darkened by years of sweat, hung around his neck. Renee walked past, crossed Frances Street, and spun to get a second look. He was gone.

Chapter Thirty-One

Renee and her parents reached a compromise about counseling: if Renee complied with her parent's curfew, got straight As on her progress report, stayed in school all eight periods every day, and spoke with her guidance counselor when she felt anxious, she would not be forced to attend formal therapy sessions.

Renee enjoyed a brief winning streak. She appreciated her classes at the high school. Anthony's infatuation with the NBA provided her with some breathing room in their relationship. Gloucester High's Board of Education selected *The Little Mermaid* as the school musical, and Renee was enthused about the upcoming tryouts.

She was surprised to be nominated for her class Homecoming Court, no doubt fueled by some sympathy votes, but satisfying to a girl who wore running shoes, yoga pants, and a vintage rock t-shirt to school most days and never gave a thought to vying for anyone's attention. Her Homecoming Court photo was displayed with the other nominees' photos in the school foyer. Each time her mom picked her up from play rehearsal, she felt delight in seeing Renee's photo in the display case. Other girls in the Homecoming display were dressed to impress and beamed bright smiles. Renee looked somber and wore a light blue t-shirt that read, "Just Passing Through." Nevertheless, Renee's selection gave her mom hope that life was returning to a happier, more carefree time.

Renee enjoyed finding a grey skater dress at Lulus to wear to the dance.

"I like the way it accents my flat chest," Renee told her mom.

"Honey, you're only fifteen. Aunt Louise was flat as a board until junior year and look how busty she is."

"That happens to me, I'll kill myself."

"Renee!"

"I'll have them lopped off."

"Renee!!"

"I like me just the way I am, mom."

"I like you just the way you are, too, honey," her mom said.

The turmoil of summer receded. On Friday, Renee competed in a band competition at Pitman High School. Following the competition, the band bus dropped the Gloucester High kids off at the high school, and Renee strolled to King of Pizza with her friends. Their silliness quickly exhausted her, so she walked home. When she was passing the pine trees at Martin's Lake, the old man was sitting on the same bench smoking another cigarette. She walked over and sat next to him. They sat in silence for a minute, staring at the lake.

"Should I be afraid of your presence in my little city?" Renee asked.

"I'm your ally," he said.

"I saw you in a vision back in August. You helped me leave a note for my friend. Why are you here now?"

"People intend to hurt you."

"Present tense 'intend' or past tense 'intended?'"

"Both."

"And how do you know this?"

"I can feel it."

"What is your name?"

"Jose Ruiz."

"You've come here from Mexico to alert me."

"To help protect you."

"Are you a shaman? Did you know Ana?"

"I made a devil's bargain with Ana because my nephew was in danger."

"Did she keep her end of the bargain?"

"My nephew was freed from prison."

"What was your end of the bargain?"

"You."

"You're the medicine man Ana spoke to on the phone while she held me captive."

He resumed staring into the lake.

"You are innocent and naive," he said. "There is much that you don't understand. My body is worn out, like an old sweater. My soul will shed it eventually, perhaps sooner rather than later. I want to assist you before I pass."

"How can you assist me?"

"That is up to you. If you wish, I can prepare an antidote to restore you to who you were before taking the potion from Ana."

"What if I don't want to be restored?"

"Your decision. Then I will teach you the ways of the warrior. I will be here tomorrow evening at twilight."

Renee turned to reply but he was gone.

Chapter Thirty-Two

A watchman found the bodies of Renee's abductors in the Philadelphia warehouse. The discovery created hysteria in the local and national media. Since the massacre on the set of the *Savage Skins Show*, national media outlets provided major coverage to the wolf-related incidents in the Philadelphia area. There were websites devoted to the wolf attacks. News magazines gave increased print space to each new occurrence. Comedians developed routines centered around the attacks. The *National Enquirer* put the story on its front page with the headline: "Year of the Wolf." Rumors abounded that a Hollywood producer had green-lighted a screenplay based on the attacks.

"I'm assuming it was you who caused that commotion in Philly," Anthony said when he picked up Renee for school.

"Remember that day I didn't come into school until the afternoon? Those guys abducted me on my way to school and took me to the warehouse in South Philly. I relished the thought of eliminating them. It was when the police were guarding my house. After I did it, I filmed the dead bodies and texted it to the cartel people in Mexico. I was hoping it might deter them. But now I worry that they might just send another crew up here after me. And I worry that I'm placing the people close to me in jeopardy. You. My parents. My friends. They're not going to care about collateral damage. I'm feeling confused and alone. Eventually they're going to kill me."

"Don't even say that, dude," Anthony replied. "I thought you were looking forward to being this badass avenger. Sounds like you're having some doubts."

"If the cartel would disappear, I'd accept a fate of protecting innocent people. I'd accept any danger that came with that. I could avenge the hurts of the innocent."

"Don't think the cartel is going to disappear. Making them disappear from Gloucester would be good," Anthony replied.

"I met an old man at Martin's Lake who can help me. He knows about the dilemma I'm in."

"A wolf guru?"

"Don't be funny. He's the medicine man who made that stew for Ana."

"And now he wants to protect you? Sounds shady. Wish Jerome was around."

"I'm at a crossroads. I can go back to the old Renee or I can accept the changes and learn to optimize them. My past, present, and future are coming together. He's capable of restoring me to the girl I was before I ate that stew. But if I do that, I'm completely vulnerable to the cartel attacks. I'd be dead already without these powers. To complicate things even further, he's ancient and he's wearing down. He compared his body to an old sweater that has too many holes in it to keep you warm. So the offer is now or never. I can change back, or I can learn the ways of a warrior."

The old man was sitting on the same bench in the same clothing, smoking an unfiltered Camel. Renee sat next to him and kicked away some small, decayed tree branches so she could put her feet on the ground. Darkness was descending. Neither of them spoke, but the silence felt comfortable and relaxed. He lifted his hat and ran his fingers through his coarse white hair.

"I need your guidance," Renee said. "Evil people in Mexico sent five men up here to kill me. They abducted me on my way to school. I attacked all five of them, so they're no longer a threat to anyone, but this is not the life I want. I have no peace. I'm also afraid I'm putting my loved ones in jeopardy. I would die if my parents got hurt because of me. I've hurt them enough emotionally. I'm grateful for your offer to help me."

"Motivated by regret," he said, "but not even a sorcerer can change the past. I wish to be a benefactor to you. You have extraordinary powers. You are much more powerful than the three men who came here to assist Ana. Their powers were waning. Your powers can expand. A deep commitment is required to understand them. There is an internal cohesion to our powers and they must be studied before you will fully appreciate them. It's best if you understand all that you are capable

of before you return to battle."

"How long will I have to study them before I fully realize them?" Renee asked.

"Fifty years."

"*Fifty years?*"

"At the very least. You must know your own heart before you can begin to

understand any of them."

"Meanwhile, my short-term goal is to survive until my sixteenth birthday."

"You must approach the new non-ordinary reality with the same devotion,

respect, and self-assurance that you approach the study of ordinary reality in the

classroom. You've accepted the labor of learning in the classroom. Now you must

accept the toil of this learning. You have great inner strength and will continue to

be blessed with great knowledge. You must fortify your heart. Have you realized

anything so far?"

"To allow the transformation to occur rather than try to force it. To become

willing to be transformed causes the transformation. Additionally, I become

invisible when I transform. I walked alongside these hikers in the Pine Barrens and

they weren't aware of my presence. I walked close to people in a park in

Philadelphia and they didn't notice me—and I was close enough that I could feel

their body heat." He nodded slowly and looked at Renee. He had remarkable eyes.

"Let's go to that park in Philadelphia now."

"Should I contact Uber?"

"You have gifts not yet realized. Be willing to be transported. Let your thoughts dissolve. Make your mind still. You can arrive without traveling. Still your mind and imagine yourself in that park."

Renee meditated and let her eyes focus softly on the lake. After thirty seconds, she shook her head and said, "I can't stop thinking. I'm wary of you. Part of me wants to remain on guard."

"We are sitting on a bench in the center of your hometown. Your thoughts are the threat, not me. Quiet your mind. Imagine being where you want to be, the park in Philadelphia. When the agitation in your mind stops, you'll arrive."

Renee breathed slowly. Her thoughts calmed. When she opened her eyes, she was sitting beside the old man on the cliff paths in Fairmount Park between the Philadelphia Museum of Art and the Fairmount Water Works.

"Amazing. What else can I do?" Renee asked.

"Lesson one: Remain mindful that you can die. You are powerful but not invincible. Let your death be a constant companion. I will wait for you in the little park two days from now. Reflect on this lesson," he said, then disappeared.

After a frantic minute, Renee calmed herself and returned to Gloucester.

Chapter Thirty-Three

Philadelphia has a hundred unsolved homicides each year. Homicide detectives struggling to piece together a case wrestle with hazy motives, scant evidence, inconsistent eyewitness accounts, and contaminated crime scenes. The Philadelphia Police Department assumed that the wolves who caused the mayhem at the *Savage Skins* shoot in Society Hill also killed the attacker in Fairmount Park and were responsible for the havoc at the warehouse in South Philly. The police didn't realize that the diableros were killed at the parking lot with Ana. That a Mexican woman was blown up in a rental vehicle was puzzling until detectives discovered that Ana was related to the head of a drug cartel. The number and caliber of bullet casings at the scene further supported the theory that Ana was killed in a drug deal gone bad.

The two men executed at the Third Base Lounge had long criminal histories. Police at the scene assumed they had been murdered by other criminals from the Philadelphia underworld. The fact that Jerome Brailey had vanished led investigators to speculate that he may have been killed, too. Investigators initially thought the deaths at the Third Base Lounge were related to the never-ending war over drug distribution channels in Southwest Philadelphia. However, a forensics detective matched fingerprints from a spent bullet casing from the August killing at

9th and Callowhill to one of the men found slain at the Third Base Lounge. Law enforcement personnel were stymied.

Another loose thread that puzzled law enforcement officials was the disappearance of Class A Investigator Diego Gonzalez of Mexico's Federal Ministerial Police. Mike Scher of the FBI was particularly troubled by Gonzalez's disappearance. Scher thought Gonzalez was a police officer of great integrity, character, and intelligence. Gonzalez's absence haunted Scher enough that he called Chief Moran and asked to meet with him and Detective O'Brien at Dolson's.

"Still can't believe how crazy things were this summer," Scher said.

"Glad those wolves are no longer roaming the 08030 zip code," Moran said. "But Gloucester's not completely out of the woods. About a week ago, two strangers were around here asking about the young girl who was kidnapped, Renee. We were worried they might be cartel enforcers connected to the lady who drove the black van. Thought they might want to squeeze Renee about who killed her. We had cops guarding Renee's house for five days, but we never heard from them again."

"Got your appetite back, Chief?" Scher asked.

"He's making up for lost time," O'Brien said. "Every meal's Thanksgiving dinner again for the Chief. Hope you got paid recently. Might be an expensive lunch."

"I appreciate you both taking the time to meet with me. Gonzalez's disappearance disturbs me. It's really troubled me. He was exceptional. Completely on point at all times. Smart and insightful," Scher said.

"What do you think happened?" O'Brien asked.

"He was supposed to be part of the security detail transferring the cartel leader to Brooklyn. Never showed up. Left all his clothing and personal belongings in his hotel room. Left a substantial amount of cash, too. Way more than he ever earned being a Mexican police officer."

"There you go. So he had a secret life that we didn't know about. I don't know any cops that carry bags of cash around with them," O'Brien said.

"Did he seem despondent or ever talk about any personal troubles?" Moran asked.

"No. He said his job was satisfying and challenging. He felt like he was making a difference."

"Did he leave his cell phone at the hotel?"

"No. I had our tech people check his cell history while he was in Philly. Nothing out of the ordinary until his final call. Only personal calls were to family members in Mexico. But his final call bothers me. A woman called 911 from Gonzalez's cell phone the day Gracias was transferred to Brooklyn. A woman used

Gonzalez's phone to report the dead body at the 9th and Callowhill Street parking lot."

"Weird. Think he had anything to do with her death?" Moran asked.

"Don't know. The Philadelphia PD report says a lot of shell casings from military-grade weapons were found in that parking lot. The woman, Ana, was blown to bits. Whoever wanted her dead *really* wanted her dead."

"Any hunch about what she was doing there?"

"My guess is that she had a drug operation planned and it went to shit," Scher said. "Her brother was neck deep in the drug trade. Maybe she was striking out on her own. But why here? Why Philly? She was the cartel leader's sister, not a foot soldier."

"Did she have a criminal history back home?"

"No criminal history. Worked behind the scenes, they told me. Was a fixer for her brother."

"Any history with Gonzalez?"

"I doubt it. Different generations, different sides of the law," Scher replied.

"Money corrupts even good people if they're in a desperate situation. For all we know, Ana could have bribed people down in Mexico to have Gonzalez sent here to be her eyes and ears on this side of the law. Not accusing the guy, but stranger things have happened. Gotta admit that it looks suspicious that the call to report

Ana's killing was made from Gonzalez's cell phone. How would he know about it if he didn't have anything to do with it? Plus, you said he had a lot of cash with him. Sounds like he was dirty," O'Brien said.

"Did anyone ever interview the young girl after she returned home? She was held captive by Ana? Maybe she knows something," Scher said.

"She couldn't have been with Ana at 9th and Callowhill or she'd have been blown up with her. She's been through enough. We'd have to have some concrete evidence before I'd even consider questioning her," Moran said.

"She's struggling with enough already," O'Brien offered. "She's having adjustment problems, as you might expect."

"Do me a favor?" Scher said. "If you ever have any dealings with her in the future, ask her if she ever heard or saw Ana speaking with Gonzalez? And let me know either way. I'll be forever wondering what happened to the guy."

Chapter Thirty-Four

Mike Scher returned to the FBI field office. Moran and O'Brien drove back to the police station on Monmouth Street.

"I don't think we should bother Renee Sears," O'Brien said.

"No way. She's been through enough. The woman who kidnapped her is dead. Case closed," the chief said. "It's crazy how Gonzalez just vanished. But there's an infinite variety of ways humans can screw up. The fact that he had a bag of cash in his hotel room…. Maybe some harm came to the man, or maybe he's shacking up with a stripper he met at Delilah's."

O'Brien delivered some paperwork to the city clerk's office, then drove to Anthony's house. Anthony was sitting on his front steps, playing video games on his phone. O'Brien got out of the patrol car and sat next to him.

"How are you doing, Anthony?"

"Doing pretty good. Doing better in school."

"Did you get any progress reports yet?"

"Just got our first one."

"How'd you do?"

"Pretty good. Two Bs, two Cs, and two Ds."

"You must have more flexible standards than me, buddy. My old man would have slapped me in the head for a report card like that."

"I usually start the year off with all Ds and Fs. I've been trying to keep my mouth shut, for starters. Doing most of the work. It's a good start for me."

"Tell you what. You get rid of those Ds by the next report card, I'll get you a hundred dollar gift certificate to one of the sneaker places at the mall."

"Well, your money's probably pretty safe, but I appreciate the offer."

"Are you planning to go out for the high school basketball team?" O'Brien asked.

"No. I'm what they call a 'gym class all-star.' Never actually played for any of the school teams."

"Why is that? You love basketball more than anybody I know."

"I missed the boat. The kids on the high school team have been playing organized basketball since they were eight years old, even younger. Nobody ever signed me up for anything. I didn't know youth sports existed. I never played organized sports because my home life was never organized."

"That's a shame."

"It'll be different for my kids. I'm going to sign them up for everything. Take them to practice. Watch all their games. I play basketball down on the courts along Johnson Boulevard. Think there's a certain level of stability required in a family to do more than that. I never had it. It's not like I'd have been the next LeBron. I'd be an average high school player. Probably playing on the junior varsity another year or two and then playing varsity senior year. I'm not all that athletic. No big deal."

"Might have been fun though. You would've maximized your potential. Gloucester High has some good coaches."

"Yeah, it does."

"Listen, I know you're close with Renee. She ever mention anything about a young Mexican cop being involved with that lady Ana? You don't have to tell me any details. I'm curious about him because he was up here working on the case and then he disappeared."

"Is this completely off the record? Just two friends talking on the steps?"

"I will never bring it up again in any context."

"I saw that guy in the chief's office one of the days I came to the police station looking for you, remember?"

"That's right. He was there."

"I can tell you this: he was working for that lady Ana."

"That's a fact?"

"Put it in concrete, dude."

Chapter Thirty-Five

Gloucester High's Homecoming Dance was held on Saturday, October 27. Young girls had their hair styled by Katie Reader or Sam Lindsay. They got their nails done and their eyebrows threaded and tinted. They argued with their friends about where to go after the dance. Boys picked up flowers at Sunshine Flower Shop or Erin's Secret Garden and made last-minute runs to the mall for socks, dress shoes, or a tie. Renee was excited about wearing Sole Society flats with her grey skater dress. Anthony planned to wear dress pants and a shirt he bought at Forever 21 with a pair of Timberland leather shoes. He had just taken his second shower of the day when his cell buzzed.

"Well, well, well, well, Anthony, how are things in—Yvonne, what's the name of that town y'all were spying on that lady in?"

"Gloucester."

"Anthony, how are things in Gloucester? It's Jerome."

"Heyyyyyy. Doing pretty well. Heading to the Homecoming Dance with Renee in about an hour."

"How she doing? Hold on a sec. Yvonne wants to talk with you."

"Hey, little man. How are you?"

"I'm good, Yvonne. Glad to hear your voices. We were worried about you after

Renee saw that story about the stuff at the Third Base Lounge. We were afraid it was you and Jerome."

"I've been better, but I'm doing all right. Don't want to say too much over the phone. The stuff at Silky's is a terrible mess. We are back in the area for a little while. Turns out we weren't suited for beach life. Jerome is bad company no matter where I take him. We're staying at a hotel on your side of the river for a couple of nights. Crossing the bridge right now. Any chance we can talk with you in person for five or ten minutes? Want to pick your brain a little."

"I'm taking Renee to Homecoming tonight. Remember Renee?"

"Honey, I ain't forgetting Renee if I live to be a hundred. Think you can squeeze out of the dance for five minutes? I'll call you and we'll meet you in the parking lot. Hoping you might remember a detail or two I can't recall. What's the theme of your Homecoming?"

"I don't know."

"Guess what the theme of my Homecoming Dance was? 1990 Strawberry Mansion High School in North Philadelphia? The theme was 'It's A Family Affair.'"

Jerome and Yvonne began to harmonize,

"It's family affair,

It's a family affair…"

"Good music never goes out of style, does it, Anthony?" Yvonne asked.

"I gotta go. My uncle's giving me a ride to pick up Renee, take some pictures, and drop us off at the dance. Call me later and I'll come out to the parking lot."

"We're going to stop somewhere and grab a bite to eat. Our two old brains can't remember certain important details from the summer and I'm hoping your young brain can. Won't take but five minutes. Enjoy the company of that precious young girl and enjoy the dance. See you in an hour or two," Yvonne said.

Chapter Thirty-Six

The scene at Renee's house was lighthearted and joyful. It briefly felt like the ordeal of the summer never happened. The kids posed for photos. Renee's parents were relieved to see that Anthony's uncle was a responsible adult. Renee's aunts and cousins made a fuss about her dress, her shoes, her hair, and the corsage Anthony gave her. The pure-hearted innocence of both teens was on full display.

"First time I saw you without your running shoes," Anthony said as they walked down her front steps to ride to the high school.

"Don't get used to it," Renee said. "I feel like a ballerina."

"You look beautiful."

"You look like Brad Pitt. You even smell good for once."

"For once? What's that supposed to mean?"

"It's your sneakers, Anthony. No big deal. Half the boys in the high school have that same musty scent. Boys' sneakers should come with an expiration date. You smell great right now."

"Thanks for the vote of confidence."

"Can you dance in those Tims?"

"I could have two cinderblocks on my ankles and if a good song comes on, clear some space on the dance floor, dude. I'll be dancing all night if the DJ's any good."

"Are we going to slow dance?"

"I've been working on my Ed Sheeran footwork all week."

"Thanks for being you, Anthony."

"I'm the total package, dude."

The high school is a short drive from Renee's house, and before long they were dancing to a remix of Meek Mill's "House Party." The dance was held in the high school cafeteria. After spending an hour with her whirling dervish of a boyfriend out on the dance floor, Renee was ushered to the high school gym to have yearbook photos taken with the other members of the 2017 Homecoming Court.

Anthony was drinking a soda with some of his friends when his cell buzzed. It was Yvonne.

"We're at your high school, Anthony. Which side of the building is the dance in?"

"Drive around the right-hand side of the school," Anthony explained. "You'll see the lights on in the cafeteria. Park in the back. I'll be right out."

Anthony walked to a car parked in the shadows along the football field fence. It was the only car on the lot with tinted windows. Yvonne lowered her passenger-side window.

"Who is this guy? Look like a movie star. Hop in the back for a quick minute."

Anthony climbed in the back seat of a new Infiniti QX50.

"Jerome, the first time I laid eyes on this young man I thought he was homeless. Now he looks like he's going to the Grammys," Yvonne said.

"How's my main man doing?" Jerome asked.

"Pretty good. Having fun with Renee."

"Help me out for just one minute. Two close friends of mine were killed over at the Third Base Lounge last week. What I don't know is if the killings are a payback for the trouble this summer or if it's an old Philly grudge getting settled. Anybody on this side of the river asking any questions about the mayhem from the summer?"

"Two dudes from Texas kidnapped Renee on her way to school one day. They took her to an abandoned warehouse in South Philly where three other guys were waiting. They tried forcing her to say who killed Ana."

"Cartel people. That's what my instincts told me. What did Renee say?"

"Let's just say those men didn't make it back to Texas."

"I hear that. All right, my man. Have fun and stay safe. Thanks for clearing that up," Jerome said.

"See you, Jerome. See you Yvonne."

"So long, honey," Yvonne said. Anthony returned to the dance.

"Think they were the same guys who killed Lee and Snap?" Yvonne asked.

"Nope. People don't hang around after committing a crime like that. After they made the mess at the Third Base Lounge, they disappeared. I will guarantee that. These are hit-and-run crews. Expendable riff-raff trying to prove themselves to the cartel. Bet the cartel sent another team up after Renee. The cartel has enough money to hire half the rednecks in Texas. Bad thing is, they were looking for us. Thinking Atlanta might be a good place to lay low for a while. Lotta good rap music come outta Atlanta. Maybe I'll get a piece of that action. Bankroll some youngster and hope he hits it big. I specifically told all those guys to stay away from the Third Base Lounge. Thinking those thugs Ana showed me might come up here looking for me."

"You gave at least five people the key to the place, Big. Those guys aren't disciplined enough to stay away," Yvonne said.

"Let's stop at that Wawa we passed on Market Street. I'm in the mood for a Gobbler," Jerome said.

They pulled out of the high school and seconds later pulled into the Wawa parking lot.

"Want a Gobbler?" Jerome asked.

"We ate dinner an hour ago. How are you even hungry? I'm going to stretch my legs. Been in this car all damn day," Yvonne said.

Yvonne gazed at the darkened soccer filled across Market Street. The steady

202

flow of headlights blinked like fireflies in the foreground. Yvonne scanned the left horizon, hoping Anthony and Renee were enjoying their evening.

"Excuse me," a voice said, drawling out his vowels like they were being poured with molasses. "You from around here?"

Yvonne stared at a man with a grey, coarse mustache, his neck blotchy from a too-tight starched collar.

"Hereabouts," she replied.

"I'm with the press," he said, holding out what appeared to be a library card from Brownsville, Texas. "We're trying to arrange an interview with the girl who was kidnapped by the wolves this past summer, Renee Sears. Wouldn't happen to know where she lives, would you?"

"Came all the way from Texas to interview a little girl from Jersey? Didn't realize the story had traveled that far," Yvonne said.

"It's the wolf angle that makes it fascinating," he said. "My partner and I," and here he pointed in the direction of a Chevy Silverado, where a middle-aged man in a Longhorns cap saluted her with a bottle of Gatorade, "are looking to do a feature length article on her for the *Brownsville Bugle*."

"On a Friday night at nine o'clock?"

"Looking to establish where she lives tonight. We'll stop by and talk with her folks in the morning."

"Well, I don't know where Renee lives but my boyfriend's the mayor of this little hamlet. He'll be out shortly. He knows where everyone lives. You can follow us over to Renee's."

"Much obliged, ma'am. I'll hop back in the truck and we'll follow you when the mayor comes out."

Jerome strolled out thirty seconds later, waving a sandwich bag at Yvonne like it was a winning lottery ticket.

"Slipped a five dollar bill across the counter at the young man making my sandwich and asked for a little extra cranberry sauce and filling. Mmmm. My mood is on the up escalator," Jerome said.

"Jerome, gimme the keys. I'll drive. Tip your sandwich bag to those two cowboys in the Silverado over there and get into the passenger seat. Tell you why in a minute," Yvonne said.

Jerome received the same Gatorade bottle salute as Yvonne. He buckled his seatbelt and said, "What's the story, morning glory?"

"Those two cowboys are looking for Renee. One of them showed me some dumbass library card, claiming to be a reporter. They from Brownsville, Texas."

"How we gonna isolate them?"

"They think they're following us to Renee's house. I'll take them down to the river end of town near where Ana was staying. There's a bunch of dark empty spaces by the river. You got a weapon?"

"As always. Got a Glock 26 in my waistband. There's a lightweight Ruger under your seat. Why don't you throw it in your purse next stop sign?"

Yvonne drove down Market Street to King Street with the Texans right behind.

"Left or right?" she asked Jerome at the stop sign.

"Let's go left," Jerome said. There was a park on the right side of King Street that led to the Delaware River, but it had a security gate blocking vehicular traffic after dark. On the left side of King Street, two wood-framed houses sandwiched a produce business. The business had a warehouse in the back and a side parking lot.

"Pull into this lot," Jerome said. "Make them think she lives in one of these places."

The Texans pulled into the lot behind them. To their right was a house with pale yellow siding. On the left was an office with "All State Produce" stenciled on the front window. The business had a second-floor apartment with a one-step entrance from the middle of the parking lot. A warehouse with an aluminum overhead door was behind the apartment. Behind the warehouse was a carport that sheltered a twenty-foot cut cabin fishing boat, in storage until spring.

"I got it from here," Jerome said.

They shut off their engine and exited the car. The Texans followed suit. Lights from the park across King Street bathed the lot in a dusky glow. One of the Texans extended his hand.

"Mr. Mayor. Everyone in this town as agreeable as you? Which place is the girl's? We can take it from here."

"Least I could do figuring you guys never been to these parts before. Am I right?"

"Never been in New Jersey. Had a little business in Philadelphia a while back."

"Business didn't involve torturing two Black men, did it?"

Jerome pulled his handgun to his hip.

"What are you talking about?" the man demanded.

"Open up that tool box in the truck cab."

"Why you trippin', partner? Ain't nothin' in that toolbox besides tools."

"I'm gonna put a third nostril in both your heads in a second. Preemptive strike, I like to call it."

Yvonne held the revolver on the men while Jerome patted them for weapons. Each man had a pistol. One of them had a Smith and Wesson finger actuator knife in a sheath on his ankle.

"All the reporters down in Texas armed to the teeth? Or just you two? What do you want with the little girl?"

"Gonna ask her a couple of questions and get right back on the highway."

"Open the fucking tool box."

"Fuck you."

Jerome shot him.

"Open the toolbox, cowboy," Jerome told the second man.

"Fuck off."

Jerome shot him.

Jerome and Yvonne dragged the bodies into the carport. They removed their cell phones and the keys to the truck and hoisted the bodies onto the boat.

"Want to see what's in the tool box?" Yvonne asked.

"I know what's in the tool box," Jerome said. "The tools they used to torture Lee and Snapper. I put two and two together before we left the Wawa parking lot. These guys were skunks. Felt it in my gut. Trouble is, it don't take a lot of skill to kill a man, and they're just gonna recruit two more once these rednecks don't show up back in Brownsville."

"What do you want to do with their truck?" Yvonne asked. "Truck's going to draw attention by tomorrow morning."

"Gonna drive the truck over to the Third Base Lounge. Gonna throw the redneck's wallets with the credit cards and money still in them on the floor of the truck and park it right in front of my bar. Let everyone know that Jerome 'Bigfoot' Brailey still wielding that terrible swift sword of vengeance. They'll find the bodies over here soon enough and figure out what transpired. Word'll get out on the street that I still handle my own problems. Make anybody in Philly think twice about fucking with me."

"I'll follow you over to the Third Base Lounge."

"Let me grab a pair of gloves so I don't leave any prints on the truck. We can go through their cell phones back at the hotel."

Chapter Thirty-Seven

Jerome parked the truck in front of the Third Base Lounge. He placed both wallets on the floor of the truck with the men's driver's licenses, credit cards, and money still in place. He wiped down the doors, steering wheel, and seat and hopped into the car with Yvonne and rode to their hotel in Cherry Hill.

"Likely to see a steady stream of Texans until this mess is put straight. Too risky sending a Mexican across the border with a weapon. Plenty of people would draw the wrong conclusion in this political climate. Only, in this case it would be the right conclusion."

"We ain't about to take on the cartel?" Yvonne asked.

"Gonna be a string of cowboys from Brownsville, Beaumont, Corpus Christi, Galveston. People working on this side of the Gulf for the cartels," Jerome said. "After we go through their cell phones for contact information, use one of their phones to call the Philadelphia PD and tell them where the truck is. Don't mention the bodies in the boat. They'll find them soon enough."

"How they gonna connect them to the truck if the truck's in Philly and the bodies are in Jersey?" Yvonne asked.

"Guarantee they both been to prison. Cops will ID 'em through fingerprints or dental records. Least we avenged Lee's and Snap's deaths. Put this on my tombstone: 'He never harmed an honest man.'"

"How about this? 'He was annoying to the very end.'" Yvonne said.

"Worst thing about these cowboys being from Brownsville is that it ruins the town's vibe for me."

"Why would you care about Brownsville, Texas's vibe?" Yvonne asked.

"You never heard 'Smokin' in the Boys Room' by Brownsville Station? My theme song during junior high. Guilty pleasure of mine. A lot of brothers only listened to soul and R&B. Not Jerome. I love White music too."

"Stop right there. I'll buy you breakfast tomorrow if you promise not to sing that song."

"Too late now. Singers gotta sing. 'I was smokin' in the boys' room…'"

"I'm begging you, Big."

"Text that Anthony, will you? Set something up where we meet him and his friend for dinner tomorrow. Gotta figure out how to respond to this craziness. Otherwise, there's gonna be a steady stream of hired guns pokin' around here looking to kill us," Jerome said.

"You have a plan?"

"I'm gonna have one. Mr. Silk's is radioactive. Can't go near the place. They're killing a dream of mine."

"Gonna have to be a dream deferred for now," Yvonne said.

210

"I see a way, Yvonne. I see a way. Text Anthony and let's get some sleep."

The following day, Jerome, Yvonne, Anthony, and Renee met for dinner at Max's, a restaurant on Burlington and Hudson Streets in Gloucester. Jerome slipped the hostess a fifty dollar bill and asked to be seated in the "back of the back of the back section," citing privacy issues with Renee. She refused to accept his money but took them to a side room along Burlington Street.

"So how was the Homecoming Dance?" Yvonne asked.

"It was great," Anthony said.

"Real nice," Renee added. "Should have seen Anthony all dressed up."

"Should have seen me rapping along to 'Dreams and Nightmares,' Jerome. The whole dance floor was shouting the song," Anthony said.

"Heard you got picked for the Homecoming Court, Renee," Yvonne said.

"Yes."

"Lotta times the teachers deduct points for your date. Anthony had to be a pretty big liability. Might wanna think about trading up for next year," Jerome added.

"The kids vote at our school, not the teachers," Renee said.

"Good thing," Jerome said. "At my high school, the teachers voted. I could have brought Halle Berry and she wasn't getting picked."

"Wonder why," Yvonne said.

"All right. Gonna teach you youngsters a cagey move for when you're using a restaurant for a meeting. Always tip first. Tip them before they even take your order. That way they don't care how long you linger. Tip them as much as they'd get for three tables," Jerome said.

The server came over to take their drink orders and Jerome handed him a hundred dollar bill.

"That's the tip, my man. I always tip first when I think we might be lingering a bit. You get paid first. We're in no hurry and we need some privacy."

"Sure. Wow. Take all the time you need. I'll get your drinks and wait a little while to take your order. Would that be good?"

"Perfect. Thank you very much for the courtesy," Jerome said.

"Always a gentleman, Jerome," Yvonne said.

"You won't need charm school after hanging with me for a while, Renee," Jerome said.

"He's annoying, Renee, but he does have certain charms," Yvonne said.

"Sounds like Anthony," Renee said.

"All right. Let's get down to business," Jerome said. Jerome was wearing a Bathing Ape hoodie and a Philadelphia Eagles baseball cap. "Don't want to cast a shadow on your Homecoming weekend, but that drug cartel sent two cowboys up here last night with every intention to harm you, honey."

"Where are they now?" Renee asked.

"On a highway to hell. Put a bullet in both of them," Jerome said. "What's most aggravating is that they'll just send two more when these guys don't show up for roll call tomorrow."

"I'm grateful we're talking about this. I realize how powerful the cartel is, but we have to figure out a way to stop them," Renee said, "or else someone else could be harmed, like your friends at Silky's."

"You're playing my song, darlin'," Jerome said.

"What can we do about it?" Anthony asked.

"Preemptive strike. Go on the offensive."

"What are you thinking, Big?" Yvonne asked.

"Renee, you still capable of doing that little magic trick you showed us at the Third Base Lounge after we freed you?" Jerome inquired.

"To the nth degree," Renee said. "I understand my powers better."

"Don't talk about anything you don't feel comfortable talking about. Fewer people know what you're capable of doing, the better," Jerome said.

"I'm all in," replied Renee. "I've acquired powers even Anthony doesn't know about yet. I'm trying to keep that part of my life separate from our friendship."

"Well, he can be excused from the table if you want. Anthony, don't you have some homework to finish?" Jerome asked.

"Yeah, all right, Jerome. I do about as much homework as you used to do," Anthony joked.

"I'll explain things to the best of my understanding," Renee said. "I don't mind Anthony knowing. I try to keep that part of my life separate because it throws our relationship out of balance. After a while, it's all we talk about. So I keep that part to myself."

"I saw with my own eyes how much Anthony cares about you, Renee," Yvonne said. "Not sure if he ever tells you this, but I saw how he loves you and values you. Saw that over the summer."

"He has his moments," Renee said, her eyes sparkling.

"Just the way I roll, dude," Anthony said.

"Now that we got the family therapy session out of the way, let's get down to the real nitty-gritty," Jerome said. "Acknowledge that we are lucky to still be standing on top of the dirt and not sleeping under it. But good luck don't last. Matter of time before one of us gets it."

"Anthony, this stuff stays at this table, all right?"

"You have my word, as always," Anthony said.

"'Til death do us part," Jerome added. "Now let's hear what you have in your

214

artillery, Renee."

"I'm more powerful than those other wolves. Still mortal, still vulnerable to anything that will kill a wolf. Keep that in the front of your minds—my mortality."

The server returned to take their dinner orders. After he was out of earshot, Renee continued, "I'm fast. Usain Bolt fast. Strong, quick, powerful. Every strength those first wolves had, mine are significantly heightened."

"Bad to the bone," Jerome said.

"My mind can make my body invisible. I can be brushing against someone's leg and they won't see me."

"You can be walking right amongst whoever you're after and they can't see you?" Jerome asked.

"Right. And that's not all. I can teleport my body anywhere I want. I sit quietly somewhere and enter a meditative trance and then move myself to distant places."

"Some Star Trek shit right there," Jerome said.

"You better be true blue, Anthony," Yvonne said. "Renee catch you steppin' out on her and you hear some growling, get down on them knees and beg forgiveness, son."

"Glad none of my old girlfriends had any of this," Jerome said.

"Wouldn't have made it out of seventh grade, Big," Yvonne said.

"How old are you?" Jerome asked.

"Fifteen."

"You keep honing these skills, imagine what a force for good you can be," Yvonne said.

"I'm trying to figure all of that out," Renee said.

"The same sweet and tender flower you were before all of this," Yvonne added.

"I'm still Renee Sears. Somewhat braver and more confident than before. But that could be the result of enduring the kidnapping. I've definitely toughened up on the interior," Renee said. "I was worried for a while that my physical appearance might change, but Anthony assures me it hasn't."

"They picked you for the Homecoming Court," Yvonne said. "Been sitting here wondering how Anthony ever landed someone as beautiful as you."

"Had to be a bit of a reach, Anthony," Jerome said.

"Lot of it has to do with my charm," Anthony said.

"He's loyal, smart, funny, and handsome. I know how lucky I am," Renee said.

"And I'm grateful every day, dude," Anthony replied.

"What's the name of this place again?" Jerome asked.

"Max's," Anthony said.

"Is Max's open on Mondays?"

Anthony asked the hostess.

"They open at three, and it's 'Mussels Monday,'" Anthony said. "Five dollar plates of mussels all night long."

"That settles it," Jerome said. "Let's meet here tomorrow for dinner. Next time, Yvonne can pick up the check. Give me twenty-four hours to devise a game plan. Tired of looking over my shoulder and I've only been back a few days."

"Tell me about it," Renee said.

"I'll run my plans by you. Veto anything that doesn't feel right. Anything you don't feel comfortable with gets scrapped. I've been in the vengeance game a long time," Jerome said, "See you all tomorrow at five."

Renee and Anthony walked half a block to Ottie's. Jerome and Yvonne lingered at Max's.

"Whatever you do, Jerome," Yvonne said, "do not put either of those kids at risk."

"The only risk is to not attack. If we don't settle things right now, Renee's days are numbered. Invisible or not invisible. Space traveling or not space traveling. Sooner or later, they're going to send their A team. You know how it is. First you send the guys who are expendable anyway. Then you send the cocky guys, the braggers, guys trying to make a name for themselves. When the clowns don't make it back, you send your soldiers, your mercenaries, guys who have done these jobs before. You and me, we could walk away now and retire to Europe. All I'm losing is the Third Base Lounge. Renee is going to lose her life if we don't come up with a plan to scare off the cartel."

"Have any ideas?"

"We're doing this for Renee. But for starters, I'm no match for the cartel. A Philadelphia street gang versus the cartel? Bet on the cartel. For second starters, you and Anthony are not about to take on the cartel. That leaves us with an army of one—Renee. She's a threat to any of them. That might make them think twice. She's also a threat to the kingpin in the federal penitentiary. She can do a lot of damage. They would have to put a lot of their manpower and effort on stopping her. I don't think they will want to do that. They're already fighting a war on multiple fronts: the law, the DEA, other cartels, the government. They perceive she's a big enough threat, they might back off. So, yes, Renee is going to be placed at risk. But she's going to be at great risk every day of her life if we don't stop them now."

Chapter Thirty-Eight

Renee received a text the next morning from Anthony. He had overslept, blaming it on a televised double overtime NBA Western Conference game that didn't end until 1 a.m., and said he would not be ready in time to walk her to school. He would meet her in the cafeteria for lunch. His absence made Renee feel vulnerable. She walked down her steps, scanned the street in both directions, and tightened the string in her hoodie to brace herself against the morning chill. She decided to vary her route, so she walked straight down Brown to East Brown, turned at Sparks Avenue onto Market, and crossed Market Street from the north side to the south side twice, weaving her way to school, hoping to elude any pursuers. She felt relief when she walked into the music room to practice an a cappella version of Shakira's "Hips Don't Lie" for the upcoming talent show. Midway through third period, Anthony texted her with his familiar "What's your vector, Victor?" The quote was from an old movie he had seen on Netflix. He sent it every time he wanted her to meet him somewhere.

"I'm in class, Anthony," Renee texted.

"Walking up Greenwood. What period are we in?"

"Halfway through third."

"You good?"

"Yes. Why are you coming to school so late?"

"Fell back asleep. Dude, you should have seen Russell Westbrook last night."

"Anthony, I'll see you at lunch. I'm doing a lab."

They met an hour later, each of them balancing trays of food on one arm and their backpacks on the other shoulder.

"Were you okay walking by yourself this morning? Sorry I messed up."

"You didn't mess up. You do me a favor every day waking up early to walk with me. I always appreciate it. Glad you got to sleep in on a weekday."

"No scary Texas dudes harassing you?"

"No, but I was nervous. I took a different route and crisscrossed Market Street a couple of times. I don't want to live this way. Hope Jerome has a remedy."

"He's the man with the plan, chica. One of my heroes. Doesn't have any superpowers but he's smart as anything and has gigantic balls."

"Think we really can put a stop to the cartel seeking revenge?"

"Jerome's gonna come through. We'll know in a few hours."

"I worry that the only way to end this nightmare is for me to leave."

"Leave? Where would you go?"

"I've thought about it but that's not a solution. I'd die without my parents. It would be unbearable. And I'd die without you. The cartel is probably powerful enough to bribe someone to track my phone, read my texts, keep track of my movements that way. I'd have to completely cut myself off the grid. Impossible for a fifteen-year-old."

"What's Jerome call it? A preemptive strike? Scare them away."

"Is it even possible to scare cartel members? They're hardened and crazy."

"Even crazy people are afraid of wolves, dude."

"Are we walking home together after school?"

"Yeah. We can hang at Ottie's until it's time to meet Jerome and Yvonne."

Jerome and Yvonne were already seated when Renee and Anthony arrived at Max's at four. Jerome was wearing a vintage Brian Dawkins Philadelphia Eagles jersey, and Yvonne wore a Think Pink Fletcher Cox jersey. The restaurant played music from a Blue Note jazz radio station.

"Know who this is?" Jerome asked them as they approached the table, pointing his index finger toward the ceiling speaker.

"Please don't respond," Yvonne pleaded. "Ignore his question. Ask him a question of your own about the menu or our hotel or anything to avoid another trip down memory lane recreating an entire recording session."

"Yvonne, let me teach these youngsters something. This was a 1964 session recorded by the great Rudy Van Gelder featuring Lee Morgan on trumpet, Wayne

Shorter himself on tenor sax, McCoy Tyner on piano, Reggie Workman on bass, and Elvin Jones manning the drums, and I do mean 'manning' the drums. Cat sounds like he has four arms. Album was called *Night Dreamer* and was Wayne Shorter's debut on the Blue Note label. This song was written by Wayne Shorter. Think it's called 'Black Nile.'"

"You put them both to sleep, Big. Their eyes are droopy. Ask the server if he's got any smelling salts."

"It's all right," Renee said. "I love music. So does Anthony."

"I love music, too," Yvonne said, "but I don't need to know who was banging the tambourine in every song that comes on the radio. Jerome can't name ten American presidents, but he knows the engineer, studio musicians, producer, and marijuana dealer for every record made since 1960. Man wears me out."

"Yvonne, hope you don't mind me getting right down to business," Jerome said.

"Anything that takes your mind off music is good with me," she said.

"Good to see you youngsters. Renee, the day you took care of the problem at the warehouse in South Philly, did you happen to salvage any of the cell phones?"

"I still have the cell phone that they used to call the man in Mexico," she said.

"Bingo, bango, bongo. Mind if I borrow it? Want to open a line of communication with them."

"Sure. I gave it to Anthony to hide for me. My parents are on full alert. If they found it, I'd have a hundred questions to answer."

"Anthony, please tell me you saved it," Jerome said.

"Always got your back, dude," Anthony said. "I can give it to you when we finish eating."

"Excellent. Renee, did these guys get a look at you? Were you on FaceTime or Skype or any of that fancy stuff?"

"No. It was a cell phone just sitting on top of some old phone books. Audio only. No visual," Renee said.

"Just a steady stream of good news from my young friends. So no one down there knows what you look like, correct?"

"Correct."

"And I have the cell phones of those tweakers who were up here looking for you Saturday night. Between the three phones, we should be able to establish contact with somebody calling the shots down in Mexico. The jackals directing these jackasses."

The server approached to take their orders. Conversation began when he disappeared into the kitchen.

"We're in good shape. No one knows about either Yvonne or Anthony. They don't know what Renee looks like. And I doubt Ana described me as anything but a 'very handsome Black man' so anybody they send up here is flying blind. She sent a video of me to them but I'm hard to hit because I'm a moving target. On the liability side, they know about Mr. Silk's and they can ask for Renee's address. I'm gonna avoid Mr. Silk's until we settle this, but Renee, you and your family are in harm's way."

"Sadly, yes," Renee replied.

"All the more reason to settle this right now," Jerome said.

"Could you offer them some of the money back in return for backing off?" Anthony asked.

"Sure thing," Jerome said. "We'll start with your twenty thousand. I'll put you on a plane tonight. After they stop laughing, they'll take it from you and make you a human piñata. These guys got plenty of money. It's an honor thing. They won't stop until we make it unpleasant for them to continue. And that's where Renee comes in."

"You okay, honey?" Yvonne asked.

"I'm good," Renee said. "The only way out is through. I'll do whatever it takes to get back to a normal life."

"If I determine exactly where these guys are, can you teleport down there?"

"I think so. I've never done it farther than Philadelphia, but I'm sure it's the same principle."

224

"And you're ready to go to war?"

"I'm ready to take my life back from the people who stole it from me."

Chapter Thirty-Nine

For the past twenty years, Esteban Gracias had lived a life of maximum consumption, his every indulgence satisfied by the profits from trafficking cocaine, methamphetamine, and heroin through Juarez and the Gulf of Mexico. Now he was awakened by a mechanical horn that blared at six each morning. He was being held in protective custody. Rather than joining the other prisoners for breakfast, he ate alone in his cell after guards slipped cold oatmeal, two toasted pieces of white bread, a slab of butter, and watery pineapple juice through a slot in his cell door. He lived in a nine-by-nine-foot cage where he spent twenty-three hours each day. He was kept in protective custody because there were many people who would pay a fortune to have him killed. He had ordered hundreds of killings in the past twenty years. He had paid the impoverished wives of men serving lengthy prison sentences after their husbands executed a contract killing on his behalf in a prison or jail. Now he was wary of sharing the same fate. Mexican street gang members could kill him on behalf of rival cartels. He was vulnerable for as long as he was held in an American prison.

Growing or importing drugs for consumption in the United States was no challenge at all. What was a great challenge was maintaining the land and infrastructure to move drugs across the border. Gracias had been ravenous in his acquisition of the land and infrastructure and ruthless and unmerciful in his defense of it. He had hundreds of millions of dollars in various banks but wore a white t-shirt, an orange jumpsuit, and a pair of cheaply made sandals. His cell contained a toilet, a six-foot bed platform with a thin mattress, and a table bolted to the floor. The table held a sheet, two blankets, a towel, two pairs of men's underwear, and two pairs of white socks. He was taken to a prison yard one hour a day to exercise. The hour varied each day to thwart snipers. He had powerful enemies. Some of his closest associates may even wish him dead to ensure he never testified against them. He took a cold shower every other day, and his lunch was a slimy meat product on white bread. His dinner each night was an unidentifiable protein, some white rice, and overcooked string beans with a pint of milk. He prayed for the opportunity to be extradited to the Puente Grande prison in Mexico to serve his sentence.

Gracias was not physically powerful. He was middle aged, slightly paunchy, and suffering the slowing of reflexes that comes with age. He survived by his wits, by his willingness to eliminate all perceived threats and enemies, and through protection by elite former Mexican soldiers trained in counterinsurgency tactics by former Israeli special forces commanders. His protectors were as brutal as their employer. In the American prison, he had no protection.

Despite all these indignities, he remained optimistic. He had dozens of criminal lawyers fighting for him. He was spending millions of dollars hoping that his stay

in the United States prison system was brief. Being sent back to Mexico to serve

his sentence seemed realistic to him at this point. His optimism preserved his

sanity. He had gotten his way at every juncture these past twenty years, and he saw

no reason his money couldn't purchase him the chance to serve his sentence in

Guadalajara. Back in Mexico, he would have access to round-the-clock

bodyguards, fine food and liquor, women, cell phones, and every amenity he

desired in a large private cell, sequestered away from all other prisoners. It was

only a matter of time, he told himself. For the past twenty years, it had always been

only a matter of time.

Gracias had no access to the outside world while he was held in Philadelphia.

He learned of his sister's futile attempt to free him after he was transported to

Brooklyn. The news was crushing. He had suffered the losses of many people close

to him: a brother, close friends, nephews, bodyguards, two uncles. The carnage

was collateral damage for aspiring to a life none of them could have dreamed of as

children. The loss of his sister crushed him. How many times had he told her not to

trust Americans? She had distanced herself from his business from the very start

but served as a trusted adviser in times of turmoil. She loved him always. She

laundered money for him, convinced the bishop to allow their brother to have a

Catholic funeral after the parish priest refused, arranged for private schooling for

228

his children, made real estate purchases for him; she could handle anything that did not involve violence. Gracias knew how desperate she must have been to attempt such an exercise in futility in Philadelphia. He'd heard about the shaman, the wolves, the Philadelphia gangsters, and her death in a desolate parking lot. Never trust Americans. He had preached it to her over and over. When his Mexican attorney told him that his lieutenants thought that Ana was murdered and the American police covered it up by claiming she committed suicide in her frustration to gain his freedom, he shook his head and said, "I believe that Ana would kill herself if her plans had been thwarted. She did not like this world very much. It's plausible that she blew herself up. She did not enjoy life, she endured it. She was smart and resilient but did not possess the instincts of a warrior. Her love for me made her reckless."

His attorney told him that his lieutenants had hired two crews from Texas to settle the score in Philadelphia.

"And?" Gracias asked.

"They've been unsuccessful so far," his attorney said.

"We are fighting a war on too many fronts already. Those Texans are idlers, loafers, and drug addicts. Tell Miguel to stop wasting my money and my resources simply to satisfy his anger. All our energies are to be used to protect our business in Mexico. No more crews to Philadelphia."

Chapter Forty

Some Sinaloans enter the drug trade at a young age, harvesting poppies for farmers growing opium in the Sierra Madre Mountains. Poppy cultivation has doubled in the past five years because the demand for heroin in the United States has doubled. Purple and red poppy blossoms blanket the creek sides and gorging crevices of the mountains with fat, opium-heavy bulbs that are the raw materials of the billion dollar heroin trade. The poppies are cultivated and refined into opium paste and then converted to high-quality heroin. An acre of opium poppies produces up to ten kilos of opium gum. It takes ten kilos of opium gum to make one kilo of heroin. Sinaloans who grew up in tin-roofed shacks have become rich through a combination of work ethic, cunning, intelligence, and ruthlessness. The demand for heroin is so strong that poppy plantations have become the surest bet for Sinaloan farmers to make money, even with the threats of government-run eradication programs and crop seizures. The Sinaloan poppies are refined into high-grade white heroin for distribution north of the border. Americans hooked on pharmaceutical opiates have turned to heroin as a cheaper alternative to Oxycontin. A kilo of opium paste sells for two thousand dollars, quadruple what it sold for a decade ago. A kilogram of heroin sells for eighty thousand dollars in the United States. The profit margin is staggering. Mexico is now the main provider of heroin sold in the U.S.

The cartels have seized control of the entire production chain from small-plot opium growers and heroin lab processors to street distributors in Los Angeles and New York City. After the opium paste is processed into heroin, it is transported across the border in cars, trucks, and trailers. Clandestine airstrips in mountain forests allow the cartel to move opium out of the remote mountain area quickly and efficiently. And as lucrative as the heroin-producing business is, the real key to drug distribution riches is controlling of the distribution routes, many of which were used to move cocaine and marijuana in previous decades. Whoever controls the distribution routes controls the market. The Gracias cartel controlled all facets of the heroin trade, from the cultivation of opium poppies to the maintenance of all major distribution routes in the state of Sinaloa.

Jose had lifted an assortment of hair from Renee's jacket when they sat together in Fairmount Park, correctly assuming the hairs were hers, her friends, and close associates. The hairs belonged to Renee, her parents, Anthony, Jerome, and Yvonne. Jose added a strand of his own hair, cupped the hairs in his palm, and dropped them into a duffle bag that contained a million dollars American cash that Ana had given to one of the diableros. Jose hid it for him until he returned from the work he'd do for Ana in Philadelphia. Jose shook the duffle bag vigorously, ensuring that the hairs touched as many of the bills as possible. He removed his worn leather necklace, knelt, and placed his amulet in the bag of bills. After chanting an incantation, he slipped the amulet back over his head and held his hands over the bag in supplication, kneeling and requesting protective energies from the spirit world. He then took some copal resin extracted from a Burseraceae tree in the mountains in central Mexico, poured the resin into a Mayan clay bowl, lit the resin with a wooden match, and wafted the smoke over the duffle bag. He set the bowl on the floor, prostrated in submission to the spirits until his forehead touched the clay floor tiles, and prayed for guidance and strength.

He arrived at a heavily guarded safe house in Culiacán that the cartel used as a base for their smuggling operations. Well-armed security guards with AK-47s, known as "goat horns" by the narcos because of the curved bullet clips, stopped him a hundred yards short of the property's exterior.

"What do you want, old man?"

"I have a million American dollars to return to the Gracias family," he said, gesturing with the large duffle bag in his left hand.

"Let me see," one said, unzipping the bag and peering inside. "Where the hell you'd get all this money?"

"It is money from Ana. I am returning it to the Gracias family."

The guards patted him down and told him to follow them inside. "Always on Time" by Ja Rule blared a stereo in the basement. Black combat vests and ammunition clips were stored along the far wall. A group of men watched television in a room at the back of the house. The guards explained Jose's presence, and a man in a striped polo shirt beckoned for Jose to follow him up a flight of steps and into another living space on the second floor. He gestured for Jose to sit on a wooden conacaste dining chair in the center of the room.

"What have you got, old timer?"

"I have a million American dollars to return to the Gracias family."

"How'd you get ahold of that?"

"Ana came to visit me. She asked me to arrange an introduction to three shape-shifters who she hoped would assist her in freeing her brother from a detention center near Philadelphia."

"Maybe you can explain to us what went wrong with your plan," he said. A half dozen other narcos had entered the room and watched the interrogation.

"I know nothing of the plan," Jose said. "I provided one service: to secure the services of the diableros for Ana. I was not privileged to hear the details."

"Ana took three million dollars to secure their services. Where's the other two million?"

"Two of them took their money. One asked me to hold it until he returned. He never returned."

"Lemme see the bag." He tossed the money around the bag with his right hand while holding it with his left, pulling it closer and digging his hand deeper into the cash. He walked to the side of the room and dumped it onto the floor, pulling the opening of the duffle bag as wide as he could, shaking the bag until the final bill tumbled to the floor. He ordered the other men to place the money on the table, and each of them grabbed an armful and dumped the cash until there was a mountain of cash on the table top.

"This begs the question, old timer—if no one returned from the operation, where's the other two million dollars? I don't buy your story. Ana said she was giving you the money until they returned from Philadelphia. I've wondered about this money many times, but I didn't know where your little rathole was located. Now that you've been stupid enough to come down here, how about we take a ride back and pick up the other two million?"

"I came here with deliberation and an intention. Your organization is still creating mischief in Philadelphia trying to kill innocent people."

"We have been trying to kill the people who double-crossed Ana. I believe in taking an eye for an eye."

"I subscribe to that philosophy also. Any further violence against the innocents will not be experienced by them; it will be experienced by you. If five years passes and no further violence has been directed toward the girl, I have arranged for the remaining two million dollars to be delivered to you."

"Five years? How about five hours? Will that seal the deal?" He pulled a handgun from the back of his waistband and waved it at Jose. "You're going to hop in the back of a car and lead my men to your rathole."

"An eye for an eye, and a tooth for a tooth," Jose said, grabbing the duffle bag from the floor. He began to replace the bills from the table into his bag.

"Can you believe the balls on this guy?" he asked his confederates.

Jose retrieved a lemon wrapped in damiana leaves from a pouch at the bottom of the duffel bag. He spun toward the narcos.

"I have a grenade. I am going to leave with the money. I will toss the grenade at anyone who follows me." He walked to the door, then pivoted quickly toward the narcos, hoping to draw fire. Three of them shot at him and immediately fell to the floor, bleeding and screaming. Five others stood in disbelief, their mouths agape.

"I will repeat what I said earlier," Jose said. "Anyone who attempts to harm the innocent near Philadelphia will experience the consequences of their violence. She is under my protection."

Four bodyguards, alarmed by the gunfire, charged into the house.

"Hold your fire," the man in the polo shirt said.

Jose walked slowly through the doorway, through the courtyard, past another phalanx of security guards, and into the town center. He found the offices of Esteban Gracias' lawyer. He was the only attorney in the country who had never dealt with immigration issues, business formations, commercial litigation, compliance regulations, environmental taxes, or real estate. He had one business interest and one client. The attorney had grown up in family that worked the shipping end of the cartel's drug enterprise. He showed great academic promise at an early age and was sent to college and law school by Esteban Gracias for the expressed purpose of working exclusively on eliminating legal challenges for the Gracias cartel. Jose was stopped and frisked by an armed guard before he was allowed to enter a handsomely decorated waiting room. Two secretaries, the lawyer's sisters, were so absorbed in typing that Jose had to knock on the top of the Formica countertop to get their attention. He asked to see the attorney, saying he had money he wished to return to the Gracias family. The attorney came out immediately and led Jose into his office.

"You the guy who just left the compound?"

Jose nodded.

"Please come sit down. What is your name, sir?"

"Jose Ruiz."

"Look, Jose. Ana was desperate enough to believe your folk magic could free her brother. It couldn't. It was a last-ditch, misguided effort borne of love."

"What you call 'folk magic' can do many things," Jose said.

"This is the end of the show. The Gracias have no plans to return to

Philadelphia. You have my solemn word. We are not looking to settle any scores or hold any inquisitions. These latest forays to your area were ordered by hotheads at this end and carried out by freelance cutthroats from south Texas. No more. That order comes from Esteban himself."

"I have the money Ana left for the men she hired. They never returned, and they have no families."

Jose put the duffle bag on the attorney's desk.

"There's not going to be any bats flying out, is there? I bear you no grudges, and I have an excess of trouble already."

Jose stared at him and sighed. The attorney unlocked the duffle bag, peered inside, and said, "You're an honest man. Thank you for taking the trouble to return the money. You're a man of honor. Please believe me when I tell you that this is the very final contact we will ever have with you or any of your allies."

He extended his hand. Jose shook it lightly and returned to his pueblo along the Sonora River. This was the final dealing he or Renee ever had with the Gracias cartel.

Chapter Forty-One

Three days later, Jose Ruiz waited for Renee at the little park around Martin's Lake. Jose was sitting on a bench under a grove of evergreens, his back straight, his expression serious and expectant. When he noticed Renee, his expression softened, as if a slight relaxation was an appropriate signal that he had recognized her. Renee greeted him, and he nodded his head.

"It's been peaceful up here the past few days. We've been trying to devise a strategy to counter the hostility from the cartel," Renee said.

"The cartel is no longer a threat to you," Jose said.

"In what way?"

"In any way. They have come to an understanding that it is a waste of their time and resources pursuing vengeance in Philadelphia or Gloucester."

"Should I believe them?"

"Yes."

"My ordeal is over?"

"The cartel is no longer a threat. That threat has been extinguished. Your ordeal is just beginning."

"It's an enormous relief that the cartel will no longer attempt to harm me. Thank you," Renee said, crying.

"You must have an unbending intent to learn all that you can about your new powers. Do you have unbending intent?"

"Yes, I want to learn everything I can. I'm just relieved that people are not trying to kill me."

"You are the 'escogido,' one who is chosen," Jose said. "Different from ordinary people. You chose the power and the power chose you."

"When did I choose it?"

"Before you were born."

"Why me?"

"You possess a certain disposition of character. You have already proven yourself. You've performed deeds of an extraordinary nature. Now you must continue to gain knowledge."

"I'm willing," Renee said.

"Do you have any questions for me?"

"Who am I?"

"You are a diablera."

"No!"

"You are a girl who knows how to become a wolf, a diablera. There are many secrets of power and knowledge that you must continue to unravel."

"Are you a diablero?"

"Yes. I am a sorcerer. You are a warrior. Continue to defy fear. You did not stop even when you were afraid. That is the mark of a warrior. You must develop the clarity of mind to prepare for a life lived with deliberateness and truthfulness."

"And I volunteered for this?"

"You could have spent your life living in ordinary reality if you had taken the antidote I prepared. It was your final test. You accepted a destiny of living in both ordinary and non-ordinary realities. Learn to assimilate some of your powers for use while you are in human form. I once killed a man with a single blow of my arm. There is a crack between the world of diableros and the world of men. Use your dedication to acquiring knowledge to become wise enough to draw meaningful inferences from each of your experiences."

"Will you be my ally through all of this?"

"We are connected both in this life and the life to come. But the path you must travel is meant for your feet alone. You came into this world alone and someday you will exit it alone. The knowledge you gain will be gained on your own. Some things are true for a single set of eyes. If I sense you are in danger, I will use my powers to assist you."

"I am honored and humbled," Renee said. "Thank you."

"I am honored and humbled also. Farewell."

Chapter Forty-Two

Renee and Anthony walked home from school the following day. An early November chill was in the air. The sky was grey and a misty drizzle was falling from the skies. Renee was excited that the Gloucester High music department was taking the singers and musicians to New York on Wednesday to see a Broadway musical. Anthony was excited that Thanksgiving break was on the horizon.

"Will you please text Yvonne and ask if she and Jerome can meet us at Max's this evening?" Renee asked.

"Getting used to eating pan-seared salmon, right?"

"Wrong. I have some news I want to share with them."

"You're taking me to the NBA All-Star game? That's really nice of you, Renee. They'll both be happy for me."

"I'll watch it with you on television. That's the best I can do for now," she said.

"I was watching this Animal Planet show about wolves last night and they were talking about how alpha wolves groom their replacement alpha because animals are not afraid of dying like we are. Interesting, right?"

"Really fascinating. I met with the shaman Jose last night. I didn't tell you because I'm still digesting the information myself. I'll explain it to you once I make some sense of it. But some of the stuff is pertinent to Jerome and Yvonne.

241

Will you text her?"

Anthony texted her and she promised to meet them at Max's in an hour. Renee texted her mom to say she would not be home for dinner "for a sensible reason." Her mom protested mildly but reiterated her trust in Renee.

"You know what's funny?" Renee said as they walked past the post office on Broadway. "My mom's trust level increases if I say I'm with you. It used to be the exact opposite. One time during the summer, my mom told me she wouldn't believe you 'if the Twelve Apostles were standing there vouching for you.'"

"Wow. Glad her opinion of me changed."

"Yes. Now they trust you completely. For a while they trusted you more than they trusted me. "

They sat at Ottie's for a half hour and then walked the short distance to Max's. Anthony wore the same great Philadelphia 76'ers hoodie the wore every day. Renee wore her Pink hoodie to ward off the chill. Jerome showed up in a Notoriouss hoodie and a baseball cap with four emojis on it. Anthony immediately begged him to trade hoodies.

"What makes you think I'd wear that Sixers hoodie after you've worn it the last twenty-four times I've seen you?"

"You've seen me like five times, dude."

"And every single time you were wearing that beat-up hoodie. Surprised you'd even give it up. Can't imagine what it smells like. Walk me to the car after we eat and I'll give you this hoodie. You can keep the Sixers hoodie. Ain't followed them since Allen Iverson left."

They ordered dinner and talked about the weather changing. Jerome was proceeding with his plans to renovate the Third Base Lounge, once again hoping for a Thanksgiving Eve reopening. He said he'd have guards posted at the door and at the parking lot gate.

"You're not looking for work, are you, Renee? Have to say you'd be the absolute state-of-the-art in personal protection details."

"You won't need me. That's what I wanted to speak with you about. I met with the man from Mexico last night, Jose Ruiz. He's taken care of the problem. They pose no further threat, he said."

"He say if he knows this for a fact, or was he just talking to the wind?" Jerome asked.

"He met with narcos and he met with Esteban Gracias' attorney. They both understand it is futile to continue to battle with us. They agreed."

"Did he use any of his magic to drive home his point?"

"He is a sorcerer."

"So you're assuming he did. Cast some sort of spell on 'em or something…"

"He said they won't risk coming up here anymore."

"We can breathe easier?"

"We can breathe easier," Renee said.

No one had room for dessert. Jerome paid the bill and removed his Notoriouss hoodie.

"All yours, Anthony. Been real nice doing business with you two."

"Thanks a lot, Jerome. Wouldn't know how to find one of these."

"Least I can do for a loyal soldier."

"Might be our final goodbyes," Yvonne said. "Going to miss your innocence. Wish you all good blessings from this day forward."

"Great knowing you, Yvonne," Anthony said.

"Now, now, don't get too sentimental," Jerome said. "What's the legal drinking age in Philadelphia?"

"Twenty-one," Yvonne said.

"How old are you guys?"

"Fifteen."

"Six years from now, you two ever out for a night in the big city, better stop and see us at Mr. Silk's Third Base Lounge. Cause you know what they say, right? 'Gotta touch Third Base before you go home.'"

91013183R00152

Made in the USA
Columbia, SC
15 March 2018